SECRETS
AND
LIES

Also by Andrew Lawrenson:

The Brotherhood of the Star trilogy:

Legacy: Shadow Watch

Prophecy: The Dreamlands

Destiny: The Sacred City

SECRETS AND LIES

By Andrew Lawrenson

Published by Pyrian Publishing

Secrets and Lies

ISBN 978-1-910980-09-5 (Kindle)
ISBN 978-1-910980-10-1 (Paperback)
ISBN 978-1-910980-11-8 (Hardback)

Published by Pyrian Publishing
info@pyrian.co.uk

2 4 6 8 10 9 7 5 3

For Karen

"Do you know what love is? I'll tell you: it is whatever you can still betray."

– John le Carré, The Looking Glass War

*"Some men carry torches for old loves, and then some guys
– not many, but some – get completely consumed by the torch's flames."*

– Harlen Coben, Six Years

Prologue.

This was it. This was how he was going to die.

'Tell me where it is,' the man snarled in his face.

'I don't know... honestly,' sobbed John as he looked down at the floor, unable to look the man in the face.

'Your lover... she kept her silence even as I tortured and killed her.' John's head snapped upwards as his brain processed the words. 'Yes,' the man hissed. 'I took great pleasure in taking her life myself. So really, there's no reason not to tell us. When it comes down to it, I don't believe you will have quite the same strength that she had.'

'Please,' begged John. 'I don't know where it is.'

'Bring her in,' barked the man, and an accomplice stepped out through the open door. He returned a moment later dragging a chair back with him, two legs scraping along the floor. There was someone sat in the chair, hand-cuffed to it, but even though there was a cloth bag over her head, John could still tell who it was; the shape of her body, her clothes... the wedding ring on her finger.

The man who had dragged her in pulled a pistol from his belt and readied it. Then he slowly raised the gun, holding it to the side of her head.

'How many people that you love have to die before you tell me what I need to know?' the man in front of John whispered into his ear.

'No, not my wife, *please*,' he whimpered. 'She doesn't know anything. She's got no part in this.'

He just shook his head slowly.

'I don't know where it is,' John repeated, slowly and clearly.

'Three,' said the man as John squeezed his eyes shut, unwilling and unable to witness what was about to happen. 'Two... one...'

John heard a deafening gunshot ring out in the small room, and then the sound of his own screams.

Chapter 1.

John Garner sat in the darkness of his study. The glow of his laptop was the only illumination, the gentle patter of rain against the window the only sound. He yawned, stretching his arms and then glancing at his watch; it was almost midnight. The presentation on the screen before him was due tomorrow morning but he had been staring at the same page of words for over thirty minutes now. He desperately needed to finish it, but he was too tired to concentrate any more. He would get up early instead and look at it again first thing in the morning.

'Are you coming to bed?' called his wife, Amy, from across the hallway.

'In a minute,' he muttered as the light in their bedroom flicked off. He closed the presentation and instead opened his email, briefly checking for anything of interest. It was just the usual; endless companies trying to sell him stuff he didn't want or need, reminders about things he no longer cared about. He turned to his social media account, flicking idly through pages of updates from people he barely knew. None of it was of any interest to him, and he scrolled down without paying it much attention, only pausing momentarily as he hit a section of friend recommendations.

He was just about to turn it all off and go to bed when a name jumped out at him from the screen. Buried in the list of people that he might know was one that he actually did; Sarah Hutchinson. He clicked nervously on the name, his heart starting to beat a little faster. Her account was bare, with no sign of any activity and only the profile picture to help identify her. It was slightly blurred and out of focus, but it was definitely her. He guessed it had been taken a long time ago as she looked young, possibly not that much older than when he had last seen her.

He sat in the darkness looking at her picture as he wondered what to do. They had been young lovers a long, long time ago — almost two decades ago, when they had both been at university together. He hadn't seen or spoken to her in all that time, not since their split — a messy, painful affair that had left him in ruins for months. He knew he shouldn't. Some things are best left in the past. They had both moved on a long time ago. Still, the name sat on the screen, calling to him in the darkness, *taunting* him.

He thought of his wife, lying in bed across the hall and then slammed the lid shut on the laptop.

No, he thought to himself. *No good can come of this.*

John lay awake in bed, staring blankly at the ceiling while his wife lay next to him, snoring softly. He was unable to sleep and instead he just lay there, long-forgotten memories and emotions surging from the depths of his memory, rattling his mind and keeping him awake. He glanced at the clock next to him. It felt like he had been lying there for hours, but it had only been an hour and a half: ninety minutes of inner turmoil as he wracked his mind as to what he should do. He had an important client meeting in the morning and he knew he desperately needed some sleep, but he just couldn't relax. Every time he closed his eyes, he could see her face: those deep blue eyes and her perfect smile, framed by her long auburn hair. He wondered if she would still look the same now. Would he even recognize her?

He looked at his wife lying next to him and then closed his eyes, taking a slow deep breath. Sarah had been such an important part of his life back then, and he had taken their breakup so very badly. He had managed to forget about her for almost a decade, but now she was back and he couldn't get her out of his mind. He felt a yearning in the pit of his stomach that he hadn't felt for a long, long time.

He couldn't just lie there anymore; he had to do something. He quietly rolled out of bed, trying his best not to wake up his wife; judging by her continued snores, he had been successful. He put on his dressing gown and then tiptoed back down the hall to his study, where he sat down in front of his laptop once more. He sat in the darkness for two minutes, gathering his willpower, before he reached out and lifted the lid.

The machine flashed back into life, bathing his face in bright light and making him squint. Her name and picture were still there, glowing in the darkness and silently calling to him.

It wasn't cheating, he told himself. He had no desire to get back with her, to hook up again or to rekindle old passions. There was just so much he had left unsaid. After they had split, he had been a mess and he'd never had a chance to properly say goodbye. He told himself that he simply wanted closure.

He opened a chat window and began to type.

Hi, he began. *I saw you on here and just thought it would be nice to reconnect and see how you are. Hope you're doing well. John.*

He read the message again and again. It sounded okay – casual, without any inappropriate overtones. As his finger hovered over the send button, he thought once more of his wife. He should just delete it – delete it and carry on with his life. But he wanted to speak to her again so very much.

Fuck it, he thought to himself as he clicked on *Send*. *Too late to do anything about it now.*

He closed his eyes and then gently pulled the lid of the laptop shut again. When he opened them again, the room was dark and silent and he crept back to his bedroom, quietly crawling back into bed. The night was cold, and he nestled close to his wife, feeling the warmth of her body under the sheets. He wouldn't have thought it would come so easily, but as he closed his eyes, darkness descended and sleep gently washed over him. His mind was at ease, at least for the time being.

John awoke with a start the next morning, his alarm clock beeping at him in the darkness. He waved his arm around in the blackness until he found it, managing to press the button to turn it off. Next to him his wife rolled over, mumbling something into her pillow in her half-awake state. John needed an early start to finish his presentation for that morning's meeting, but there was a little while yet until either his wife or daughter needed to get up and get ready for their day ahead.

He headed straight for the study, opening his laptop and checking for any new messages. There weren't any. Of course there wouldn't be – it had only been a couple of hours, a couple of hours when the vast majority of people would have been asleep in their beds.

His message was still on the screen, and he looked again at the words he had typed the previous night. They looked innocent enough. There was nothing there to feel guilty about, but nevertheless he did still. It was too late to do anything about it now though. The message had been sent, and there was no way to undo it.

He left the laptop running while he went to the bathroom to prepare himself for the day, brushing his teeth, showering and shaving. With that done, he returned to his study, opening his presentation. There were only a few hours left now in which to finish it, but try as he might he kept flicking back to his messages, hoping for a reply but always coming up empty.

He spent the day in a daze. The important client meeting was a disaster; he stumbled his way through it, unable to properly focus or concentrate. In the end, his boss took over most of the talking. He hadn't said anything openly to him, but he knew that he was annoyed and disappointed with him; a lot rested on getting this client. For John, though, it was like he was a love-sick teenager again, idly daydreaming his way through life while he waited for his crush to call him back.

The rest of the day wasn't much better. He drifted through his time at the office, his mind grounded in a thick bank of fog. On the drive home, he almost had an accident, only noticing someone pulling out of a side road at the very last moment, swerving and avoiding a collision by mere inches.

He arrived home a nervous, sweaty wreck of a man.

He let himself in, calling out to his wife to let her know he was home. He took off his shoes, placing them in their correct space by the door, and hung his coat up on its hook. Then he shuffled into the living room, collapsing onto the sofa. One of their daughter's inane TV shows was blaring from the TV: something about vampires, or possibly werewolves. Maybe both.

He looked up to see his wife standing in the doorway. She had been talking to him, but he had no idea what she had been saying.

'Are you okay, dear?' she asked again.

'Huh?'

'You look kind of distracted,' she stated. She turned to their daughter, Olivia. 'Can you turn that down, please?' It was hard to think over the sounds of various creatures ripping each other limb from limb in the corner of the room.

Olivia sighed and grunted. 'I'll watch it in my room,' she muttered, gently tossing the remote control at her mother.

Amy caught it, pointing it at the television and switching it off. The room descended into silence once again. 'Is there anything you want to talk about?' she asked, coming over and sitting down on the sofa next to him.

Nothing I can discuss with you, he thought, although he made himself turn to her and smile. 'Just problems at work. A big presentation didn't go as well as hoped. I'm not sure my boss is particularly happy.'

'Nothing I can help with, then?'

'I really don't think so. This is something I need to sort out for myself.'

From upstairs, they could hear the sounds of the same TV show starting up again, now reverberating down through the ceiling.

Amy stood up. 'I need to get back to the dinner,' she said as she started to walk back towards the kitchen.

'Amy?'

'Yes?' she said, pausing on her way.

'I love you.'

'I know,' she replied in a matter-of-fact manner. 'Dinner's in about half an hour.'

❋ ❋ ❋

By the next morning John was almost back to his normal self. As he went through the day, he was checking his phone for messages less and less often, and was finding it easier to concentrate on his work. By the evening he had pretty much given up hope of hearing from Sarah, and had resigned himself to rejection once again. He reminded himself that her account had looked ancient, like it had been set up many years ago and then never used. He'd be surprised if she ever even saw his message, let alone chose to reply to it.

He returned home in an incident-free journey, letting himself in and finding his wife in the hallway. He gave her a little peck on the cheek, and she replied with a small smile of appreciation.

They ate their dinner in near silence, their daughter not even bothering to remove her headphones as she ate. Afterwards John excused himself in order to finish off a report that had been due earlier that afternoon; he supposed that tomorrow morning would have to do.

As night fell he was once again sitting in his study, working on his laptop in the darkness. He worked through the evening on the report and was just putting the last finishing touches to it when the laptop gave a little *ding* and a chat window opened up.

He felt his stomach squirming, his pulse racing. It was Sarah.

Hi, it began. *It was certainly a surprise to hear from you, but a nice one. How are you doing?*

Very well, he typed. *I'm living in Yorkshire these days with my wife and daughter.*

He felt obliged to mention them early on. He wasn't sure who he was trying to convince more that this wasn't an attempt to hook up: her or himself. He told her about his job, his family, his new life. She listened intently, explaining that she herself was single these days after a couple of messy relationships. She now worked in sales for a large multinational company, and spent most of her life on the road travelling from country to country. She was just in the country for a few days, stopping off in London to catch up at her company headquarters before she left again for a few months.

He could feel his heart beating in his chest now. He was supposed to travel to London in a couple of days to give a product demonstration to a prospective client. He was surprised his boss had trusted this to him after the last debacle, but he supposed he was giving him a chance to redeem himself. Either that or there was no one else available. It was a long journey to and from central London in rush hour and the meeting was due to finish late, so the company had booked him a hotel room for the night. Before he could stop himself he started typing into the chat window.

I've got to be in London myself on Friday night. Would you like to meet up for a chat about old times?

He knew that this was pushing his luck. This wasn't like him, arranging rendezvous with women behind his wife's back, but he was being seduced by a barrage of old memories and emotions that were bubbling up from somewhere deep inside him, memories and emotions that had been pushed deep below the surface for far too long and were now coming back with a vengeance. He sat there, staring at the screen, his heart beating rapidly, a cold sweat on his forehead. It was a couple of minutes until her reply came, but it felt like hours.

I'm not sure that's a good idea. My life is kind of complicated these days.

It would have been so easy to step back then, and things would have worked out so differently. Instead he typed frantically, the words flowing directly from his heart and side-stepping his brain.

I only want to talk. I'm not looking to hook up – almost the opposite. We split apart so awkwardly, and there are some things I've always felt like I didn't tell you. I'd find it so much easier in person, and I think it would give me a sense of closure.

This did at least have the virtue of being true. Despite all the conflicting emotions he was feeling, he did still love his wife. He knew his life was better now than it had been with Sarah. He knew that their breakup had made sense. He knew he was mad to even contemplate this. But he also knew that he desperately wanted to see her again, more than he had wanted anything for a long time.

He sat there staring at the screen, watching the time on the clock slowly change. The reply took almost five minutes to come through, but it felt like a lifetime.

Okay. Do you know the Duck and Hounds pub in Brixton?

No, but I'm sure I can find it, he entered rapidly, opening up a web search for it as soon as he had finished typing.

I'll see you there, 10 pm on Friday. Okay?

And with that, she was gone.

Chapter 2

John stepped out of the tube station and into the cold winter night. The wind was blowing strongly, but at least it wasn't raining just yet.

As he walked out onto the pavement, he looked around; beyond the crowds of people hustling along the street he could see a rank of black taxi cabs parked just a short distance down the road. He headed straight to the one at the front of the queue, pulling the rear door open, climbing in and sitting down. 'The Duck and Hounds, please,' he said to the driver, who grunted an acknowledgement to him and pulled away from the kerb.

John strapped in his seat-belt and then pulled out his phone to look at the time. It was 9:50, just about perfect; he was only a few minutes away. He hated tardiness, and hated it when people kept him waiting, so he always tried to afford them the same respect.

He was just about to put the phone back in his pocket when the screen lit up, buzzing with an incoming call; it was from a mobile number that he didn't recognize. He swiped the screen to accept it.

'Hello?' he asked hesitantly. He could hear loud music in the background from whoever was calling him; it sounded like a club or a concert.

'John?'

His heart almost skipped a beat as he heard Sarah's voice for the first time in almost twenty years. Even though she was straining her voice to be heard over the loud music, she sounded almost exactly how he remembered.

His mouth suddenly felt bone dry, his heart pounding in his ears, but he managed a 'Yes'. Barely. 'How did you get my number?'

'You're not the only person who can look people up on the internet. Where are you?' She sounded eager... or maybe anxious?

'In a taxi, five minutes away,' he replied.

'Something's come up – I'm not in the pub. Can you meet me at the Dragonfly club? It shouldn't be far from where you are.'

John leaned forwards to the taxi driver. 'There's been a change of plans. Can you take me to the Dragonfly club?' The driver nodded, flicking on his indicator and pulling a U-turn in the empty street. John sat back down again. 'I'm on my way,' he said into the phone.

'Meet me at the bar,' she said. 'And John?'

'Yes?'

'Don't be long.'

'I won't...' he started, but then realized she had already gone.

The taxi pulled up outside the club ten minutes later and John passed the driver a twenty pound note, telling him to keep the change as he hurriedly climbed out of the vehicle, slamming the door behind him.

The Dragonfly club was located on a back street in the seedier side of town. Ironically, it was quite close to where his hotel was located; his entire journey had almost been in a complete circle. This was obviously a discreet club that didn't need to advertise its presence; a small brass plaque by the door was the only clue as to its existence, although as he stood on the pavement outside he could hear the *thump-thump-thump* of bass from the music inside.

He headed for the door, and as he approached a smartly dressed bouncer nodded at him, taking a step to the side. John pushed the door open and was hit by a wave of heat and music. He ignored the sweat and the noise, the pounding bass rhythm instantly reverberating through his head, desperately pushing his way through the crowds as he made his way towards the bar.

As he neared the bar, he saw a woman standing with her back to him. He couldn't see her face, but even from behind, the colour of her hair and the shape of her body were recognizable. As she turned around, his suspicions were confirmed and he stopped in his tracks. She had a few more lines on her face and a couple of extra piercings in her ears, but apart from that she was almost identical to how he remembered her.

'John,' she called as she spotted him, her mouth forming into a smile that brought back plenty of old memories.

'Sarah,' he managed to say, almost having to shout over the music. 'Good to see you.'

'Good to see you too,' she replied, 'but we need to go.' She turned and slid a note across the bar to the barman.

'Where?'

She ignored his question, instead taking him by the hand and slipping her arm through his, leading him across the floor like they were a couple again, the last twenty years just a dream. She was heading straight for the door.

She leant into him as they walked, pushing through the crowds dancing to the music, talking directly in his ear to be heard over the noise. 'Where are you staying?' she asked.

He could smell her perfume and her sweat, and as her nose rubbed against his cheek he thought he might faint. 'In the Marriott,' he said. 'Not far from here.'

They made their way through the crowds and to the front door, which she pushed open, stepping out together into the cold night air. Three taxis were parked in a taxi rank on the other side of the road, and she headed straight for the one in the middle.

'It's not far,' said John. 'We could easily walk there.'

Sarah ignored him, opening the rear door of the taxi and ushering John inside. 'The Marriott,' she told the driver anxiously.

'I think he's due a fare next,' said the driver, pointing to the car in front of her.

'I prefer the look of your car,' she said simply. 'Let's go.'

He shrugged back at her. 'You're the boss,' he replied, and then with a brief flick of his indicator he pulled out into the road.

'Sarah,' began John, but she simply leant towards him and placed her index finger on his lips.

'Not now,' she whispered gently. 'We can talk when we get there.'

'But...'

'Shush. In a minute.'

The suspense was killing him. This was all moving too quickly, but he did as he was told, holding his tongue and keeping his questions for when they arrived at the hotel.

Sarah seemed excited, grasping John's hand tightly, occasionally looking out the rear windows. Whatever she was looking for, she didn't seem to find it. Their journey only took a couple of minutes, and then she was climbing out, slipping the driver a note with one hand and pulling John out of the car with the other.

He stopped next to her on the street, still holding her by the hand. 'Sarah,' he started again, as she looked first up at the hotel in front of them, and then left and right along the street.

With her free hand she held up a finger to her lips. 'It's cold out here – let's just wait until we're inside, okay?'

'Inside?'

'Your room,' she said with a smile, as if any other destination would be stupid. 'Come on, John.' She pulled him by the hand, leading him towards the hotel reception. He hesitated momentarily, and then let himself be pulled forwards. He had never been able to say no to her.

They strode through the lobby hand in hand, past the reception desk and straight into a waiting lift. John pressed the button for his floor and then stood back as the doors pulled closed. He looked at her as they stood alone in the lift, her face reflected left and right in the mirrored walls. This was all moving too fast for him. He wasn't sure if this was really happening, or if it was all just a fevered dream.

The lift doors opened again with a chime, bringing him out of his reverie. They stepped out into the corridor, John leading Sarah the short distance to his room and opening the door with his key card. With the door open he stepped back to let her enter but instead she waved him in.

'No, after you,' she offered, looking up and down the corridor before following him across the threshold.

'Are you looking for something?' he asked, as she shut the door behind them and then locked it.

'Just making sure we're alone,' she whispered, flashing him a wide seductive smile. She removed her jacket and handbag, hanging them up next to the door before holding out a hand to John. 'Your coat?'

'Oh. Yes.' He nervously took off his coat too, handing it to her. Even this modest level of undressing felt inappropriate, given their current location.

She took the coat and hung it up next to hers. Then she headed straight for the mini-bar, taking out two miniature bottles of scotch. Sarah cracked the first bottle open, taking a large swig of the golden-yellow liquid. She held out the other one, offering it to him. 'Want one?'

John shook his head, wincing inside at the cost of the mini-bar, but not arguing. She finished the first, and then twisted the lid on the second bottle, downing its contents.

He stared at her as she stood there. She was wearing a smart business suit; he wouldn't be surprised if it was an expensive designer brand, although he wasn't a good judge of such matters. Her long auburn hair was tied up in an elaborate design, although strands of it were now coming loose and hanging down. She still had that radiant glow about her that he remembered, and a smile that could just melt him inside. From what he could see of her arms and legs, they looked thin but also strong; she had aged very well. From the slender curves of her skirt and top, he guessed it wasn't just her arms and legs that were well toned.

He suddenly realized he must be staring, and that she was saying something. 'I'm sorry, I was miles away. You were saying?'

'I was asking you if you had anything you wanted to tell me?' She sat down on the edge of the bed and patted the space next to her. 'You said there were things you wanted to tell me, things that would be easier face to face?'

John nervously came and sat down next to her. 'I'm sorry, things have all happened so fast. I never expected to have you alone in my room... that was never my intention...'

She placed a hand gently on top of his. 'Shush,' she purred. 'I apologize for all the drama – I'll explain later if there's time.'

John looked her in the face. She still had that same beautiful smile on her face, warm and radiant, but he thought he could also detect a hint of sadness behind her bright blue eyes.

'Are you okay?' he asked.

'Just some work issues,' she replied with a shrug. 'Things haven't gone so well recently and I think I may be permanently reassigned.' Her smile widened, but it felt forced, and he definitely thought he could detect a hint of sadness in her voice. 'I may not be around much after this, so if you have anything you need to get off your chest, now's the time to do it.'

John gave her a sad grin and a little sigh. It felt strange, sitting in a hotel room with an old lover – he had always been a faithful husband, but he had also always felt able to open up and talk to Sarah. 'After we broke up, I took it quite badly,' he started, 'but that was always due to my own problems and insecurities – I never felt any resentment towards you over what happened. If I had to do it again, I wouldn't change a thing, even knowing how it all turned out.'

'No regrets,' smiled Sarah.

John started to nod and then stopped. 'Not quite. The time I spent with you was – at that time in my life – the happiest I'd ever been, but whenever I think back to our time together, it's always tinged with a hint of regret.'

'For what?'

'There were times when I was a jerk, times that make me cringe with embarrassment for what I did, times when I know I embarrassed you. But in my defence, I *was* a teenage boy, and as I have to keep reminding my daughter, all teenage boys are idiots. Horny idiots, mainly. Some are more horny or idiotic than others, but they're all horny idiots.'

Sarah gave his hand a little squeeze. 'We were both young and naive. We were each other's first true loves, and we were still learning our way, groping our way around in the dark. Often literally,' she added with a little chuckle. 'You've nothing to be ashamed of.'

John looked Sarah straight in the eyes, and she could see a tear in the corner of his. 'After we broke up I was in a very dark place, and I wasn't able to deal with you rationally; it was all too painful. I don't think I ever told you just how much you meant to me.'

'Poor old John,' sighed Sarah, running a hand up the side of his face and wiping away the tear that was crawling down his cheek. 'You meant a lot to me too. There'll always be a special place in my heart for you.'

She leaned forwards, brushing her soft lips against his.

'I'm married,' he muttered under his breath, but there was no real conviction behind it.

'Not for tonight,' she whispered back. Her lips forced his apart and then her tongue was inside his mouth, probing and caressing his. His defences crumbled, and he was hers completely.

Twice.

Chapter 3

John woke up suddenly, sitting bolt upright. The weather had worsened and he could hear the rain hammering against the window. He glanced at the clock next to the bed, which quietly informed him that it was 5:05. He was naked, sweaty... and alone.

'Sarah?' he called out softly, but there was no reply.

He stood up and checked the bathroom, but she wasn't there either. Her clothes were gone. There was no trace of her, no sign she had ever been there apart from a lingering scent of her perfume on the pillow.

He stood up and pulled his work laptop out of his bag, turning it on before heading to the bathroom while it started itself up. When he returned, he logged in and returned to his social media page. He went to his chat history, but Sarah's account now just showed as *Account Deleted*. He was unable to send her any more messages.

He fetched his mobile and unlocked it, heading straight for his call history. There it was; her call from last night. He hesitated for a moment, looking at the time on the clock. Then he called the number anyway, but instead of a ringing, all he heard was an announcement: *The number you have dialled is no longer in service.*

He collapsed back on the bed, staring up at the ceiling. She had left his life as rapidly as she had re-entered it. History had repeated itself, and once again she had left him.

He lay in the hotel bed, the bed where not so long ago he had given himself to her completely. The bed where he had felt closer to her than he had felt to anyone in a very long time – and where he now felt so incredibly alone.

He returned home later that day. His wife could tell that something was troubling him, but he just passed it off as annoyance with how the business meeting had gone. In truth, the meeting had gone well, better than could have been expected given his state of distraction, but it proved a convenient excuse.

He was still feeling troubled and confused, but the truth was that that night with Sarah had proved more cathartic than he could have possibly hoped. He wasn't sure that it was entirely due to their chat, but it still felt good to have got it all off his chest. Maybe now he could put her behind him and move on with his life.

There was still a niggling worry at the back of his mind, however. She hadn't just disappeared in the night. That would be understandable, he supposed; maybe she was embarrassed or ashamed about what had happened. She hadn't just left him – she had dropped off the face of the earth too.

No, he told himself with a shake of his head; he was being overdramatic. He wasn't the kind of man that women would abandon their life and run away over. Her phone no longer being in service... well, hadn't she said that she might be being sacked? Maybe the phone account belonged to her work. And as for her social media account? It hadn't looked like it had been used much in years – she obviously wasn't closely attached to it. She probably just felt awkward about what had happened and thought it best to break off that line of contact.

It was definitely for the best, he told himself, as he stood in the kitchen, fixing himself a drink as he watched his wife cooking dinner for himself and his daughter. He still loved his wife deeply, and was frankly embarrassed about how that night had got out of hand. He wasn't cut out for a life of secrets and lies.

Chapter 4

Over the next few days, life gradually returned to normal for John. He had been finding it hard to separate the intense feelings he had had for Sarah when he was younger with his feelings from now, but gradually those emotions were fading. Sarah had made no attempt to get back in touch with him, and without any avenue for contact, John had slowly found himself thinking about her less and less.

He still felt guilty for what he had done though; he had never cheated on his wife before, rarely even lied to her. But as he stood in the doorway of the living room, watching his wife and daughter, there was one thing he knew for certain. He loved his wife, and he resolved to put it all behind him and move on with his life.

Even his work was returning to normal. There had been another important client briefing, and this time it had gone spectacularly well. The client was interested, his boss was happy, and there was even talk of bonuses.

It was while he was sitting at his desk at work one afternoon, working his way through a lengthy technical specification for the prospective client, that his office phone rang. He reached over and picked it up, grateful for the distraction.

'John Garner,' he answered with a weary sigh.

'Hi there, this is Mandy in reception. There are a couple of men here who say they need to speak to you.'

John mentally went through any meetings he was meant to have with clients in the near future. He quickly flicked to his online calendar and also drew a blank.

'Who are they?' he replied a moment later. 'I'm not expecting anyone.'

Mandy's voice turned to a whisper. 'They say they're from the police. I think this is important.'

'Did they say what it was about?' asked John, replying in a whisper himself. He couldn't think why the police would want to talk to him. He'd never had any direct dealings with them his entire life. Well, not since he was a teenager and he and his mates had had to do a runner when they'd almost been caught drinking under age. Did he have any unpaid parking tickets? Would the police even come to your office for something like that? He doubted it. Maybe it wasn't him who was in trouble. Maybe it was his wife. Maybe she'd been in an accident. Maybe it was his daughter.

'I'll be right there,' he replied, hanging up the phone and pulling his jacket from the back of his chair.

John arrived in reception two minutes later. As he approached the front desk, Mandy stood up, tilting her head and nodding towards two men who were standing near the front door.

They were both white middle-aged men, each dressed in a dark grey suit with a white shirt and dark tie, although they were two subtly different shades of grey. They turned as he neared, seeming to recognize him, although they didn't approach and instead let John come to them.

'Mr Garner?' asked the first man, as John drew to a halt in front of them. He had a grim look on his face.

'Yes,' replied John simply. 'How can I help you? Has there been an accident?'

The second man withdrew a wallet from his jacket, flashing a warrant card at John before slipping it back into his pocket. 'I'm Detective Brand, this is Detective Watts. We're with the national counterterrorism office. We need to talk to you.'

John could feel his heart rate increasing already. This didn't sound like a problem with his wife or daughter.

'We need to talk to you about Sandy Larson,' stated Watts.

'Who?' asked John, a quizzical look spreading across his face.

'Lucy Butler?' asked Brand. When John drew a blank he tried again. 'Christine Henson?'

John just stood there, slowly shaking his head. Brand reached into his jacket pocket and pulled out a small photograph, holding it out towards John. He reached forwards, taking holding of it by the edge, but he knew what it would show before he even looked at it. It was her – Sarah. She was younger, the photograph taken maybe ten years ago, and it was grainy and slightly out of focus – as if it been taken from a distance with a telephoto lens.

'You recognize her,' said Watts. This was a statement, not a question.

John nodded and swallowed. 'Sarah,' he stated. 'Sarah Hutchinson.'

The two detectives looked at each other and exchanged knowing glances before turning back to John.

'She hasn't gone by that name for a *long* time,' said Watts.

'You must go way back,' added Brand.

'What's wrong?' asked John. 'What's happened to her?'

'Sir,' said Brand. 'Ms Hutchinson is wanted for questioning in relation to a significant number of terrorist activities.'

'*What?*' spat John.

'We have reason to believe that you're in contact with Ms Hutchinson,' added Watts.

'No. Well, yes,' stammered John. 'I saw her briefly a few days ago…'

'We're going to need you to come with us, sir,' said Brand with a sigh.

'What? No… this is all just a misunderstanding,' blurted John. He was starting to babble uncontrollably. 'I only saw her for a couple of hours; we barely talked. Look, I can show you.'

He reached into his pocket for his phone. Before he knew what was happening, Brand had grabbed his forearm, wrenching it painfully to the side and then bending it behind his back. He was shoved violently to the floor, his face smashing against the rough carpet tiles, the detective's knee in the small of his back.

'*My phone!*' protested John. 'I was going for my phone!'

The detectives simply ignored his cries and John could feel the cold metal of handcuffs being snapped around his wrists.

'You're going to need to come with us,' repeated Brand, as he grabbed John by the arms and yanked him up from the floor.

John staggered to his feet. A crowd was forming around the edge of reception. He could feel their stares, hear all the whispering. He thought his nose might be bleeding, but was unable to check with his hands secured behind his back.

Watts pulled open John's jacket with one hand, reaching inside with his other to pull out his phone. He gave a little grunt of acknowledgement – possibly even surprise – before he slipped it into his own jacket pocket. Then the two detectives took hold of one of John's arms each, marching him out of the front door. John could see the flashes and hear the clicks as his colleagues stood there taking photographs on their phones. No one said anything. No one offered to help.

They walked him down the steps to where a black BMW was double-parked in front of the building, its hazard lights flashing. Watts unlocked the car while Brand pushed him into the back, pushing his head down as he slid him in. The inside of the car was empty, almost surgically clean. It even still had that 'new car' smell.

The two detectives opened the front doors and slipped into their seats. There was a clear glass and wire mesh panel separating them from John.

'Where are you taking me?' asked John, his deep fear clear in his voice.

'Somewhere where we can have a quiet talk about Ms Hutchinson,' said Brand.

Chapter 5

The two detectives said nothing for the short trip across town.

John's heart was racing, and he could feel the damp sweat under his armpits. This wasn't good. This wasn't some minor misunderstanding and these detectives meant business. He finally broke the silence as the car pulled off the main road into a tiny side street containing the rear entrances to the nearby shops and businesses. It was only wide enough for one car to pass, its gutters littered with rubbish from large overflowing bins.

'Where are we?' he asked. This didn't look like any police station, not even the back entrance of one.

'Safe house,' explained Brand. 'We wanted somewhere quiet to have a chat.'

'If we take you to the station, then this would all have to be official,' added Watts with a smile that did little to reassure John. 'I'm sure you wouldn't want that. You wouldn't want to be officially linked with a terrorism investigation… all your friends and co-workers wondering just how involved you really are. Even if you were released without charge, they'd never look at you the same way again.'

They pulled the car into a small parking space next to some steps and killed the engine. Both detectives opened their doors, stepping outside. Brand opened the back door and leaned down to face John. 'Out,' he ordered.

John shuffled across the seat and swung his legs around, stumbling out of the car with his hands still handcuffed behind his back. Brand took him firmly by the arm, leading him up a set of steep narrow steps to where Watts stood holding a door open. The door looked strong: thick wood with a reinforced metal frame and a keypad set into the wall next to it. There was no name or number on the door, just an anonymous entrance on an anonymous street.

Brand gently pushed him across the threshold and into a dark corridor. As the door swung shut behind them, they were momentarily cast into darkness until a strip of fluorescent lights flickered on above them. They were standing in a sterile white corridor, two doors standing closed on either side.

Watts stepped past him, turning the handle on the first door on their left and revealing a dark room beyond. 'If you could...' he asked politely, gesturing to the open doorway.

John stepped forwards and into the room. This was as cold and bleak as the corridor, illuminated only by a single bare light bulb hanging from the ceiling; it flashed alight as Brand flicked the switch on the wall. A square metal table stood in the centre of the room with two plain metal chairs sitting on opposite sides facing each other. Two additional chairs were lurking in the shadows of the corners of the room.

'Take a seat,' ordered Watts.

John took a step towards the closest chair and then stopped. 'I don't suppose you can take these handcuffs off?' he asked politely. 'I'm not a threat.'

'True story,' smirked Brand, barely loud enough to be heard. He stepped forwards, slipping his keys from his pocket and unlocking the cuffs.

John heard the click as the handcuffs unlocked, then felt the pressure disappear. It felt good. He stretched his arms, rubbing at his wrists and then sat down as he had been asked.

Watts took the seat opposite him, while Brand stood in front of the door, his legs apart and his hands behind his back. He looked like a security guard guarding something of great value or a soldier guarding his post.

'We need to talk to you about Sarah Hutchinson,' said Watts. 'It's very important you tell us anything you know about her whereabouts. We need to know everything she told you.'

'What is it exactly that she's supposed to have done?'

'I can't tell you that,' said Watts. 'But it's a matter of national security.'

'Okay,' swallowed John. This really wasn't good.

'How did you meet Ms Hutchinson?' asked Watts. 'Where do you know her from?'

'It's complicated,' replied John, earning a raised eyebrow from Watts. 'I knew her when I was much younger. We were lovers for almost a year.' Brooks gave a little snort of derision when he heard this, but Watts motioned for him to continue.

'So this was when?'

'Almost twenty years ago.'

Watts looked surprised, and glanced across at Brand momentarily. 'So what's changed? Why did she get back in touch with you?'

'It was me,' said John. 'I was the one to get back in touch with her. I came across her profile on social media, and thought it would be nice to see her again.'

'You're saying you saw a social media account for her?' asked Watts.

'Yes.'

Watts sighed, shaking his head. 'I have a little trouble believing that. This woman has been a ghost for the last decade; there have only been occasional sightings, always with a different name and a different appearance, never raising her head above the parapet for long enough to be spotted.'

'She's not really the social media type,' added Brand. 'Not one for boasting about her latest holidays and what her kids have been up to in school.'

'She has kids?' asked John, looking from Brand and then back to Watts. He was still a little perplexed about what exactly was happening.

'Of course she doesn't have fucking kids,' exclaimed Watts, slamming his hand on the table. 'He was just making a point.'

'It was old,' blurted John nervously. 'The social media account was old; her picture looked like it was taken a long time ago. I was surprised when she even replied.'

'So you're telling us what? That she came out of hiding to hook up with... *you*?' Watts cast John a withering glance as he said this.

'It's not like that,' said John, desperately trying to explain. 'We were close once. We both meant something to each other.'

Brooks chuckled from his position in front of the door. 'That woman's never been close to anyone. She just uses men to get what she wants, and then casts them aside. You actually think you *meant* something to her?'

'No,' said John. 'It wasn't like that. Maybe she's not the same now, but back then…'

'So what did happen?' asked Watts, interrupting his nostalgia. He clearly wasn't interested in their relationship twenty years ago. 'What happened when you met her again? We need to know everything. Every little detail.'

'Nothing,' said John. 'Nothing of any interest. We just talked about old times.'

'We'll be the ones to judge what's important or not,' said Watts. 'Tell us *everything.*'

And he did. Starting with the phone call in the taxi, all the way up to when they kissed. He didn't tell them about her intoxicating scent, the electricity when her skin brushed against his, the look on her face as she came.

'And I think we can all guess what happened next,' scoffed Brand. John ignored him.

'And she didn't give you anything?' asked Watts. 'She didn't tell you anything about why she was here?'

'Only that she was temporarily back in London from a sales trip and was visiting her company headquarters to catch up before she had to leave again. She didn't tell me any more details than that, and I didn't ask.'

'No, I guess you had other things on your mind,' muttered Brand.

Watts stood up. 'This is going nowhere,' he sighed.

'Can I go?' asked John optimistically.

Watts ignored him. Instead he turned to Brand. 'Take him away. Put him in the holding cell for now.'

'Am I under arrest?' asked John nervously.

'Under the current anti-terrorism legislation, given that you have a clear and obvious connection to a wanted terrorist, we can hold you indefinitely without arrest,' explained Watts without looking at him, as if this was all just a matter of routine.

'Don't I get a phone call?'

'You only get a phone call if you're arrested. You haven't been arrested.'

'But I need to call my wife,' cried John. 'She'll be worried if I don't come home.'

Brand stepped over, placing his hand firmly on John's shoulder. 'Come with me, sir.'

John stood up obediently, but his legs felt like they could only just support him.'

'You need to empty your pockets,' said Watts as John turned towards the door.

John reached into his trouser pockets, pulling out his wallet and keys and placing them on the table. They already had his phone.

'We'll return them when you leave,' added Watts.

Brand led John out of the room, across the corridor and into the room opposite. This was even more spartan than the previous room – just a grubby single mattress in the far corner.

John stepped inside and heard the door close behind him, followed by the click of a key in the lock.

Chapter 6

The room was dim, lit only by a single underpowered bulb behind a wire grill. John looked at the mattress, which was stained and dirty. He obviously wasn't the first person to be incarcerated here. He was tired and scared, but he didn't want to lie down; he couldn't rest – not like this. Something was badly wrong and he was worried. No, not just worried… he was terrified.

He paced up and down the small room, running that night over and over in his head. Had she actually said anything important? Had there been any signs? She had said that she might be permanently reassigned. At the time he thought she was going to be transferred into another position at work, possibly even sacked; now he wondered what exactly she had meant. When he had first reconnected with her online, she had said that her life was complicated. She hadn't been kidding, and whatever she was involved with, now he was caught right in the middle of it too.

He had replayed that night over and over in his head many times, but now he had a different focus. He tried to recall everything she had said to him, her reactions when he had talked to her. At the time, nothing had seemed out of place, but he had to admit that he'd been completely distracted by the sight of her, intoxicated simply by her presence. Now he began to wonder why she had been in that club in the first place rather than where they had planned to meet, why she had kept giving furtive glances all around, why she was in such a rush to get off the streets and into his hotel room. Could it be that she *had* just been using him after all?

He had been replaying that night in his head for almost an hour when he heard the click of a key in a lock and the door opened. He was sitting on the floor in the corner of the room and as he looked up he saw Brand and Watts standing in the doorway.

'Stand up,' barked Watts, and he did so. Brand marched over, grabbing John by the arm and dragging him into the centre of the room, pushing him down onto his knees.

'Time's up,' declared Watts. 'We've got no more time to waste here. You need to tell us something new. Something we don't already know.'

'There's nothing,' blurted John.

John felt movement behind him and then something cold and metallic pressed against the back of his neck – a gun barrel.

'I'm going to give you to a count of five,' Brand announced from behind him. 'One.'

'I don't know anything,' whimpered John. He had known this was bad, but he hadn't expected this. He could feel himself shaking. He felt like he was going to throw up.

'Two.'

'*Honestly.* You have to believe me.'

'Three.'

'There must be something you haven't told us,' said Watts, bending down to look him in the face. 'Something you've been holding back.'

'Four.'

'I think I still love her,' cried John. There were tears starting to run down his face. He felt the metal of the gun barrel being removed from the back of his neck.

Watts stood up straight again. 'Boy, did you pick the wrong woman to fall for.' He turned to look at Brand. 'He doesn't know anything. He's useless to us.'

John jerked as he felt the cold metal on the back of his neck again. 'I hope she was worth it,' whispered Brand from behind him.

'No. Not here,' said Watts, and John felt the pressure on the back of his neck ease off again. 'I don't want to have to clean up the mess. Take him somewhere quiet to do it.'

Brand grabbed him under the arm, yanking him violently upwards. 'Come on. It's time to take a ride.'

✳ ✳ ✳

Brand dragged him back outside at gunpoint, tossing him into the back of the car before reversing out of the tight space and heading off across London at speed.

'Where are you taking me?' asked John. Brand just ignored him, looking straight ahead as he calmly cruised along the road at a steady speed.

'You don't have to do this,' he spluttered. 'I don't know anything. I'm a nobody. I won't tell anyone about her. About you. I promise.'

Brand just continued driving, oblivious to his concerns. Fear was swelling up in John now, threatening to overwhelm him. As they slowed down at a junction, John frantically pulled at the door handle, but unsurprisingly the door didn't open. He tried banging on the window, but none of the pedestrians walking along the pavement seemed to care.

'Please,' cried John. 'You don't have to do this,' he repeatedly desperately.

'If you don't shut the fuck up, I'm not just going to kill you,' muttered Brand. He kept looking forwards at the road, not even bothering to look at John in the rear-view mirror. 'After I kill you, I'll find your wife and kill her too. Not that I think you'll care too much about her, eh?'

John opened his mouth to say *No, it wasn't like that*, but shut it again. Brand didn't sound like he was kidding.

'Maybe I'll find your precious daughter and kill her as well. You wouldn't want *that*, would you?' This time he glanced at John in the rear-view mirror and John shook his head in reply.

'Good,' said Brand. 'Now shut your fucking mouth, sit back and do what I tell you.'

✳ ✳ ✳

A few minutes later, Brand pulled the car into a long and narrow road between two large industrial lots. As he climbed out, he stopped and looked around. The large walls on either side of the street were the sides of large factories, drab brick walls without many windows. It was quiet here. There were no cameras, no people, no *witnesses*.

He pulled the back door open, his pistol in his hand. 'Out,' he barked. 'Do I have to remind you about your daughter?' he added when John didn't move.

John reluctantly slid out of the back seat and stood up to face his would-be killer.

Brand motioned towards a sheltered area where several large bins stood against a wall. 'Over there,' he ordered, gesturing with his gun.

John did as he was told, taking a few nervous steps on legs that felt barely able to carry him.

'Stop,' said Brand as John neared the wall. 'Face the wall.'

John did so.

'Any last words?'

He wanted to say goodbye to his wife, tell her he loved her, tell her he was sorry. He turned and looked briefly at Brand and knew there was no point. He just shook his head.

'Well then,' said Brand, and then stopped. A white van had turned into the street and was slowly crawling towards them. Brand slipped the gun into his pocket, his finger still on the trigger, still pointing it towards John. 'No funny moves,' he muttered.

The van slowed down, creeping slowly towards them before stopping about fifty feet away, its engine gently rumbling.

Brand turned to look at the van. 'Stay there,' he barked at John.

Without warning, the van suddenly accelerated, its tyres screeching as it rocketed towards them.

'What the fuck,' muttered Brand as the van hurtled towards him. He pulled out his pistol, fumbling it slightly as he struggled to pull it out of his pocket. He briefly managed to raise the gun and fire a single shot, which went wide before he dived out of the way, rolling behind his car and scrambling away.

The van screeched to a halt, colliding with a corner of the BMW as it did so and sending it spinning into the wall in a cacophony of noise and bending metal.

In the chaos, John had fallen to the floor. From where he lay next to the wall, he looked up and saw the door of the van open. A woman jumped out and started to run towards him. Her shoulder-length hair was blonde and she was wearing tight blue jeans and a white blouse under a jacket. She held a gun in one hand.

'Sarah?' he muttered incredulously. Her hair style and colour were different, but he would recognize her anywhere.

She grabbed him by the arm, pulling him up from where he lay on the floor. 'Are you okay? We need to get going.'

'What are you...' he started to say, when Brand stepped out from around the rear of the van. His gun was gone, presumably lost when he had dived to the floor, but in one hand he instead held a sizeable combat knife.

Sarah tried to raise her gun, but Brand kicked out with his right leg, catching her by surprise and knocking the gun from her hands. It clattered off into a pile of rubbish as Brand faced her, still wielding his knife. With one hand she pushed John backwards. 'Get in the van!' she ordered, but John just stood there, staring at what was unfolding before him.

Brand lunged at her with the knife, but she side-stepped just at the last moment, the blade narrowly missing her. He tried again, but this time she was more prepared. As he moved forwards, so did she, her left arm grabbing his. She brought her right hand down hard on his arm, and the knife fell from his hand, falling to the floor between them.

That wasn't going to stop him, though. He wrenched his arms from hers using his superior strength and then took a small step to the side before swinging a powerful punch towards her. She ducked, taking a step backwards to get out of his reach.

Behind them, John had instinctively taken several steps back to distance himself from the fight, but he still hadn't got into the van.

The two combatants circled each other, weighing each other up, before Brand attacked again, unleashing a barrage of punches with both hands. Sarah brought up her arms, blocking each of the blows in turn before retaliating with a powerful kick. It made contact, but was only a glancing blow, causing no real injury other than to momentarily unsettle him. She kicked out again using her other leg, seizing her advantage. This time the blow was good, hitting him in the stomach and causing him to let out a gasp and stagger backwards.

She advanced, pouncing on him and grabbing him by the collar with both hands. She brought up her right knee, hitting him in the groin as hard as she could. This had more of an impact. He winced, the pain clear in his face, but it wasn't over yet. He punched out, and Sarah was unable to defend herself quickly enough at such a short distance. His fist hit her in the gut and

John heard her cry out. Still he just stood there watching, his mouth hanging open.

Brand punched her again, a vicious blow to her kidneys, and she staggered backwards. He sneered and took another step towards her.

Sarah dug deep, summoning all her power and fury. She struck out, her fists moving with lightning speed. A blow from her left hit him on the chin, stunning him and snapping his head to the side, before a punch from the right caught him on the other side, her diamond ring ripping a gash in his face. She stepped forwards, kicking him in the guts again and sending him staggering backwards, towards the wall and away from John and the van.

He was bent over from the blow and she leapt after him, grabbing him by the hair. She pulled him towards the wall, twisting his head and smashing his face into the red bricks – one, two, three times. He collapsed to the floor, his face and nose a bloody mess. He wasn't moving.

John couldn't believe what he had just witnessed. 'Is he...?' he muttered.

'Dead?' said Sarah, completing his thought for him. She stepped over the body on the floor, kneeling down so that she straddled him, before she grabbed his head in both hands. With a terrifying crack she gave his neck a swift violent twist and then dropped it again, where it fell to the floor with a dull thud. 'He is now.'

'You didn't have to do that!' cried John.

'You don't know who this guy was. You didn't want him coming after you.'

She rolled him over, patting him down and removing his wallet. She opened it, checking its contents: cash, credit cards and his police ID. Then she picked up his knife from the floor. She walked over to where her pistol had fallen, searching around for a moment until she found it. She gave it a quick inspection, making sure the safety catch was on and then slipped it into the waist of her jeans.

She glanced around the street, rubbing her side where Brand had punched her viciously.

'Are you okay?' asked John nervously.

'I've taken worse,' she said casually. 'At least he was enough of a gentleman not to hit a lady in the face.'

She glanced around as if looking for something, and then casually strode around the van and over towards Brand's car. She lay down on the floor, scrabbling around until she saw what she was after; reaching under the BMW she pulled out Brand's gun. She hefted it in her hand, feeling the weight, and then checked the safety, removing the cartridge and inspecting the bullets before slotting it back into the base of the pistol. 'Good,' she muttered, with the air of someone who knows what they're talking about.

'For God's sake, will you tell me what's going on,' cried John.

'In a moment,' said Sarah. 'We need to get out of here first.' She went back to the van, reaching in through the side window and pulling out a handbag into which she placed the knife and both of the guns.

'Don't I get one?' asked John.

'Have you ever killed anyone?' asked Sarah.

John shook his head.

'Have you ever even *fired* a gun? A real gun, not an air rifle or something like that.'

'No,' sighed John.

'Then I think it's best if you don't. We don't want you shooting yourself in the foot by mistake.' She gestured to Brand's car with a tilt of her head. 'I imagine your fingerprints are all over this?'

John nodded.

Sarah went to the back of the van, opening the door and removing a jerry can. She removed the lid and then started to empty the contents into the interior of the car. 'I imagine your prints aren't on file,' she said, and John nodded with a vague shrug. 'Best to play it safe though, eh?' She tossed the half empty canister into the back of the car. 'Get in the van, John.'

'Will you tell me what's going on!'

'Just as soon as we're out of here. But I need you to trust me for one moment and get in the van.'

John sighed and pulled the van door open, climbing into the passenger seat. Sarah meanwhile had found an old rag and was lighting it with a lighter. As soon as it was ablaze, she tossed it into the back of the car, where the petrol fumes immediately took hold. Then she hurried around to the driver's side of the van, climbing in and starting the engine. She floored the accelerator, the van screeching off in a spray of dust and gravel. Behind them, the car was already an inferno.

Chapter 7

'Okay, stop the van,' asked John a couple of minutes later when he felt they were far enough away. 'We need to talk.'

'I can talk and drive at the same time,' said Sarah, paying attention to the road and not looking at him. 'Feel free to talk to me, but we keep going.' She was accelerating up a slip road onto a dual carriageway. She leant out the window to check for traffic as they merged; the van had lost its wing mirror in the collision, as well as most of its front lights.

'Okay, Sarah,' began John, 'if that's even your real name...'

She gave a little chuckle. 'It is.'

'What the hell's going on, Sarah? Who were those people? Obviously, they weren't police.'

'Obviously,' she agreed.

'Then who were they?'

'I'm not sure.'

'You're not sure?' spluttered John. 'They were going to *kill* me – and almost certainly you too. What have you got yourself into, that people you don't know are trying to kill you?'

Sarah sighed as she settled the van into a steady cruise. 'I don't know their names and I don't know who they're working for, but I do know them by reputation. I believe that one back there was a Russian agent, a nasty piece of work.'

'*Agent?* Do you mean he was a... *spy?*'

'We prefer the term *agent*… or *operative*,' she said with a grin.

'So what are you? They told me you were a terrorist.'

She shook her head. 'I'm also a spy. But unlike them, *I'm* one of the good guys.'

'Then what you told me…'

She smiled. 'I was lying when I told you that I worked in sales for a multinational. That's just one of my covers. The corporate lifestyle doesn't really suit me.'

'So… you're a killer?'

'Only out of necessity. Only when I'm left no choice. Most of the time my job is actually quite boring – I don't normally spend my time running around shooting at people. You'd be surprised how much time I spend just sitting, watching and waiting.'

'And back there?'

'He was going to kill you in cold blood, John. He was all too willing to kill me too. If I'd let him live, he'd have come after both of us, and God who knows who else.'

John thought back to what Brand had said to him about his wife and daughter. He had to admit, he was glad that he was no longer a threat. 'I'm still in danger, though, aren't I?' he groaned. 'There's still the other one. He knows who I am. As soon as he finds out that Brand is dead, he'll assume it had something to do with me. He'll blame me for his death. He'll come after me.'

'We'll have to deal with him when the time comes.'

'*We?* I'm not cut out for this, Sarah. I don't want anything to do with it.'

'I afraid you no longer have much choice,' she sighed. 'I'm sorry I got you involved in all of this… but you're in too deep now. Quite frankly, if you want to live, I suggest you stick with me.'

A few days ago, spending more time with this woman would have been John's dream come true. Now, that dream was rapidly turning into a night-mare.

'What do they want, Sarah? Can't we just give it to them?'

'I can't do that, John. They can't be allowed to get their hands on it.'

'What exactly is *it?*'

'I'm not exactly sure. Top-secret information – I know that much – but the details are classified way above my pay grade. The information is en-coded onto a smart-card – you need both the card and a matching reader to extract it. It was my job to retrieve the card before it fell into the wrong hands.'

'So where is it?'

'Give me your wallet,' she asked simply.

'Why?'

Sarah sighed, turning to look at him briefly. 'Just do it, John.'

'I can't. I don't have it. They do.'

'*What?*'

'They took my wallet from me – along with my phone and keys.'

'*Fuck!*' she screamed, slamming her hands into the steering wheel. There was an exit coming up, and she swerved the van across the road, cutting across two lanes of traffic and earning horn blasts from the drivers behind her. They flew up the slip road at high speed, braking hard and then turning off at the first junction into a quiet country lane where she pulled the van up onto the grass verge.

'What is it?' asked John. 'What's so special about my wallet?'

Sarah turned off the engine. 'That's where I put the smart-card, John. The other night, before I left... I knew they'd be out there looking for me and I needed somewhere to hide it, so I slipped it between the other cards in your wallet while you slept.'

'You *what?*'

'I'm sorry, John. I was in trouble and I had no one else to turn to. If they caught me and I had it on me... if they had the card then they'd have no more need of me. I was scared for my life and I needed somewhere safe to hide it. Somewhere they wouldn't think to look. I hoped they'd never find out about you.'

'But they did though, didn't they? They know all about me.'

Sarah took his hands in hers, holding them tight. 'I'm sorry, John. You never signed up for any of this, but we're in it together now. You and me – just like old times.'

'I can't,' pleaded John, shaking his head.

'I *need* you John. I've got no one else I can trust.'

'What about your other spies? What about the rest of MI5? Surely there must be a whole department of people you can turn to.'

Slowly, Sarah shook her head. 'It's MI6, but... I'm a deep undercover agent, John. Only a handful of people know about me – the *real* me.'

'So then, we go to one of them...'

Sarah shook her head again. 'My handler... The night I met up with you, I was meant to meet up with him a few hours earlier to hand over the smart-card. I was late arriving at the location we'd agreed, and I got there only to find it swarming with police and ambulances. He had been shot, John –assassinated.'

'Fuck,' groaned John, shaking his head.

'I had an emergency contact – my handler had given me his boss's number, but when I tried to get in contact with him, I found out that he had been killed in a road traffic accident a few hours earlier. A hit-and-run.'

John slumped forwards, his head in his hands.

'You can see my problem, can't you? All my contacts, all the people who know who I actually am... are dead.'

'Surely there must be someone you can turn to? *Someone* within MI6?'

She closed her eyes and swallowed. When she opened them, John could see them glistening, the hint of a tear in one eye. 'Not without that smart-card, John. With it, I can back up everything. It proves my story – it proves who I am. Without it... without it I'm just another lunatic. Just another crazy woman with another crazy story.'

She grasped his hands tighter, pulling them towards her. 'I need you, John.' She let go of one hand, holding it to John's cheek and gently stroking his face. Then she looked him straight in the eyes. 'You're the only person I know I can trust. Of all the people in the world... you're the only one that I know for certain is on my side.'

John knew it was madness, but he'd never been able to resist her, never been able to say no to her. 'What do you need from me?' he eventually asked.

'We need to get that smart-card,' she said. 'We need to go back to where they held you.'

Chapter 8

Ten minutes later, Sarah pulled the van to a halt in the quiet back street where the safe house was located. The sun had started to go down, and it was already starting to get chilly.

John pointed out the safe house to her and they sat in the van for five minutes, silently observing the entrance. There was no car parked in the space outside and no sign of activity; no one came or left.

Sarah picked up her handbag, double-checking that her pistol was inside before she opened her door. 'Come on,' she said as she picked up a jacket from the back of the van and slipped it on. 'Let's take a look.'

Together, they quickly crossed the street and went up the narrow steps to the door. Sarah looked around; there were no obvious CCTV cameras observing them and no witnesses wandering past. She idly keyed several sets of numbers into the keypad; nothing happened apart from a small red LED lighting up below the buttons.

'Okay,' she said. 'You just keep guard. Tell me if you see anyone coming.'

'What are you going to do?'

'Just keep a look out. Okay?'

John nodded.

Sarah reached into her handbag and pulled something out – a small set of screwdrivers. She efficiently removed the screws attaching the front of the keypad and then prised it off, revealing a set of electronics within. She started poking and prodding, and a few moments later there was a buzz and the door swung ajar.

'How did you do that?' asked John in amazement.

'I didn't get this job based on my good looks and charms,' said Sarah. 'Well, not *just* on based on them, anyway.'

It was dark inside, and Sarah drew both her gun and a slim LED torch from her handbag. She turned on the torch, holding it in her left hand to illuminate the corridor in front of her. 'What have we got in here?' she asked.

'The first door on the left was some kind of interview room,' John told her. 'The first on the right was a cell. I didn't see in the others.'

'Where did you last see your wallet?'

'The interview room. First on the left.'

Sarah advanced slowly, moving as quietly as she could. As she reached the first door, she stopped and listened. The building was deathly quiet. John wondered whether the building was soundproofed – either to isolate the rooms from what was going on outside or to keep whatever happened in here a secret.

Sarah took hold of the door handle and turned it slowly. The door opened to reveal the interview room, empty apart from the chairs and table. She shone her torch around, scanning the dark shadows, but John's wallet and keys were no longer there.

'Not here,' declared Sarah. They moved to the cell next, but that was equally empty, just as John had last seen it.

Slowly they crept down the corridor together. Sarah looked at the door handle to her left. 'Bathroom,' she whispered, noting the privacy lock on the door. She grabbed the handle in her hand and twisted it. It was as she expected it: a shower and toilet, and a small sink. Basic, but clean and functional.

They turned to the final door. Sarah put her ear to it, listening intently, but could hear nothing. She turned the handle. This was a small kitchen-diner. A small oven and sink. Microwave, kettle and toaster. A small kitchen table with four wooden chairs. There was no sign of life or even occupancy. No wallet. Sarah checked the waste bin, just in case, but it only contained a few rotting tea bags.

'*Fuck*,' she swore under her breath.

'What now?' asked John.

'I don't know,' she muttered. 'I need to think.' She turned around. 'Let's go back to the van,' she sighed. 'There's nothing here.'

They climbed back into the van, and Sarah started the engine, setting off and pulling out into the main road. She headed for the A64, heading out of the city centre as rapidly as she could.

'Where are we going?' asked John.

'Just driving,' she said. 'If you just move about randomly, it's a lot harder for someone to find you.' She peered out of the windscreen into the dim dusk light. 'I won't be able to drive for long; we've only got one working side light. We don't want to be pulled over.'

She managed to get out of the city centre before the darkness of night fell, slipping into a long country lane where she found a lay-by where they could pull up.

'Why are we stopping here?' asked John.

'This is where we spend the night,' replied Sarah.

'You can't be serious?' exclaimed John.

Sarah nodded back. 'We can't get a hotel. I've got precious little cash left and all my cards are likely to trigger alerts if they're used – and you don't have your wallet anymore.'

'But I can't spend the night with you... either here *or* in a hotel. I need to get back to my wife.'

Sarah took hold of his hands. John tried to pull them free but she resisted, holding them tight. 'Listen to me.'

'But...'

'*Listen*,' she insisted. 'They know who you are... yes?'

'Yes.'

'And they know you're married? With a daughter?'

'I think so. Yes. I know they do.'

'Do they suspect that she knows anything?'

'I wouldn't have thought so. They didn't think *I* knew anything. I'm still not sure that I do.'

Sarah nodded. 'Then the best thing you can do is forget about her for now.'

'You can't be serious?'

'I'm dead serious. They're likely to be watching your house, tapping your phones. If they think she doesn't know anything then they're much more likely to leave her alone... and just wait for you to go home or contact her.'

'She won't know where I am. She'll be worried.'

'Good. If she gets worried and starts ringing hospitals, that just adds credibility that she doesn't know where you are.'

'But I can't...'

'You have to, John. If you contact her, then they'll grab her, question her... or worse.'

John shuddered. 'You're sure about this?'

'One hundred per cent positive. You have to trust me on this. This isn't the first time that things have gone sour for me.'

'So where are we spending the night?'

'Come with me,' beckoned Sarah, opening her door and stepping out. John opened his door and climbed out after her, following her around to the back of the van. She opened the rear doors, revealing the large space in the back of the van. It was empty, except for a backpack, some shopping bags containing food and water... and a sleeping bag and blankets.

'We'll freeze to death,' moaned John.

Sarah climbed inside and beckoned John in after her. 'You'd be surprised how much warmth two people can give each other.'

'Sarah...' started John.

'I know,' replied Sarah. 'But this is about survival.'

John climbed inside and then closed the door behind him while Sarah unzipped and rolled out the sleeping bag, using it like a mattress. Then she shook out the blankets, shaking them flat. John lay down on the sleeping bag and Sarah lay down next to him, covering them both with the blankets. This time they both had their clothes on though.

'That night we spent together,' asked John. 'Did it mean anything to you?'

'Of course it did, John.'

'The man you killed – he called himself Brand – he said you just used people. Used them and then cast them aside.'

She moved in closer, and John could feel her breath on his skin. 'They don't know me,' she whispered. 'You do. I think you're the only person in the world who knows the real me.'

'Then why did you give me the smart-card? Why did you drag me and my family into all of this?'

'I thought I was going to die, John. People were coming for me, and I didn't know if that was going to be my final night. Everyone I trusted was being killed. I had no idea where to go, who to turn to, but I had you. We were scheduled to meet up that night and I was sure that I could still trust you, John. If you hadn't been there, hadn't been able to give me somewhere to hide… I hate to think what might have happened.'

In the dim moon light coming through the windscreen, John could see a tear rolling down her cheek. 'I've done things in my life I'm ashamed of, things I had to do to survive or because they had to be done. But that night… that was the first night of genuine affection for a long time, John. When I saw your message, I was surprised – it was from an old account, one I hadn't used in years. To be honest, I'd completely forgotten I even had it. But I was truly glad to hear from you. When I agreed to meet you, I had nothing but honest intentions. It was only afterwards that I decided that I needed to hide the smart-card somewhere where I hoped they wouldn't find it. Somewhere safe, where – if I survived – I could retrieve it later.'

She slipped an arm around him, slipping her hand up behind his back and under his top. The warmth felt good against his skin. 'You still mean something to me, John,' she purred, 'and I think the feeling's mutual.'

'I would be lying if I said I didn't still have feelings for you,' he whispered back to her.

She snuggled down under the blankets, resting her head against his chest. He could feel the warmth of her body through his clothes, feel the swell of her breasts, smell her sweat and perfume. He ran one hand gently through her hair.

'Hold me, John,' she murmured.

He wrapped his arms around her, holding her tight.

'I loved you,' he whispered in her ear.

'I know,' she replied softly.

Chapter 9

John awoke in the morning to a cold breeze. One of the back doors was open and Sarah was sitting on the edge of the van, brushing her teeth with a bottle of water. She spat out the toothpaste onto the floor outside and then offered the toothbrush and toothpaste to John.

'We have to share a toothbrush?'

'After everything else we've shared, you're worried about that?'

John smiled. 'No, I suppose not.' He reached over and took them from her. Then he climbed out of the van, wandering down the lane to stretch his legs as he brushed. His back was stiff and sore; he hoped he didn't have to get used to this.

He looked around at where they had parked – he hadn't been able to see much the previous night. They were parked in a gravel lay-by at the side of the road, and there was a light frost covering the floor. On one side of the road he could see a small village in the distance across some fields, while on the other side he could see sheep grazing behind a thick hedge.'

'So what now?' asked John as he returned to the van.

'I need to meet up with an old friend.'

'What, I'm not enough for you all of a sudden?' joked John with a grin.

Sarah shook her head. 'It's not like that; this is purely business. Someone I've worked with in the past. He can help us.'

'If he's an old colleague, then surely you could get him to help you? You don't need me.'

She shook her head again. 'No. You'll see why,' she said with a sigh. 'Once, maybe...'

John decided not to push the issue for now. 'Okay, where is he?'

'About three hours away. We've got some driving to do.'

They set off west across the country, stopping just once to stock up on food and petrol. It was almost noon when Sarah pulled off the road into an industrial estate, cruising over towards a car workshop at the rear of the complex. She pulled the van into a parking space between two other cars, and then clambered into the back. She picked up one of the bags of shopping, emptying out the food before she gathered together Brand's gun, knife and ID, putting them into the bag.

'Come on,' she said. 'Let me introduce you to Tom.'

They both climbed out of the van and headed through the open workshop doors. There were several cars raised on jacks, mechanics toiling away underneath. A grubby young man who was leaning over an engine stood up and started to walk towards them. His overalls were covered in grease and dirt and he wiped his hands on a rag as he walked towards them.

'Can I help you?' he asked politely, looking from John to Sarah and then back again.

'I'm looking for Tom,' said Sarah.

'He's in the office,' replied the young man. 'Is he expecting you?'

'I seriously doubt it,' replied Sarah with a grin. 'But don't worry, we're old friends. He'll be glad to see me.'

She didn't wait for permission and set off towards the corner office, gesturing for John to follow. As she reached the closed door she stopped, giving it two brief knocks before entering. John followed her through to see a tough-looking middle-aged man behind a desk. He had short grey hair, his muscled arms decorated with tattoos, and a scar across his neck. He looked like he could have seen plenty of action, and John was wondering why it was that Tom couldn't help Sarah, right until the point where he wheeled his wheelchair out from behind the desk.

'Tom,' she said with a wide grin.

'Sarah...' he replied. 'If that's the name you're going by at the moment?'

'For now,' she admitted with a nod of the head.

'It's been a while,' he sighed.

'Too long.'

'So what can I do to help you? Why are you here?'

'I need some help. *We* need some help.' She gestured towards John. 'This is an old friend – older than you, even.' John extended a hand and they shook.

Tom turned back to Sarah. 'What do you need?'

'I could do with a makeover on my van outside, as well as some cash and some more *specialist* equipment. Maybe somewhere to spend the night.'

'I'll see what I can do.'

Sarah passed him the bag containing the gun, knife and ID. 'I'm afraid I don't have much to pay you with.'

Tom looked in the bag and nodded with a sigh.

'You owe me, Tom,' she reminded him softly, cocking her head and smiling sweetly. 'Don't you remember Sarajevo?'

Tom sighed again. 'I don't know,' he said with a wide grin on his face. 'Someone saves your life–'

'–twice,' reminded Sarah.

'Someone saves your life *twice*, and all of a sudden they think you might owe them something.' He peered out into the workshop. 'Is your van outside?'

'Parked out front.' She reached into her handbag and handed him the keys.

'I'll get the boys to have a look at it,' he said, as he wheeled himself out through the door.

'Was he MI6 too?' asked John when they were left alone.

Sarah shook her head. 'Independent – we both were in those days. We saw some pretty fucked-up shit together over the years. He's been out of the game for quite a long time now. Unfortunately, he hasn't got any official contacts in the intelligence community, only underground ones that aren't going to lend you or me any credibility – possibly just the opposite. Plus he's in no condition to go racing all over the country – his legs aren't the only health problem he has.'

Tom wheeled back into the office. 'Okay, the boys are going to give the van a quick makeover, fix up what they can.'

'Would it not be easier to switch to another vehicle?' asked John.

'That one's not going to be noticed for a while,' said Sarah. 'And a white transit van may not be the fastest getaway car, but it is the most anonymous. No one pays any attention to erratic driving from a white van. No one bats an eyelid if they see a white van double-parked outside their house.'

'They just assume someone's getting something delivered,' nodded John.

'And the space in the back can work out useful. No, we'll stick with the van for now.'

'I'll see what I can do about helping it blend in,' added Tom, and Sarah gave him a thankful smile. 'So what else do you need?'

'Bullets for a 9 mm Beretta M9A3,' she asked, 'and a silencer if you can manage it.'

'The bullets should be fine,' he replied. 'I'll have to see about the silencer – it might take a little while.'

'We'd need it soon, or not at all,' said Sarah.

'Well, I'll see what I can do. Is there anything else?'

'Somewhere where I could take a shower would be nice.'

'There are some bathrooms at the back of the workshop. There's a shower in there – the boys can get a bit messy sometimes. It's simple and basic… but it'll get you clean. I'll tell them to keep out while you're in there.'

Sarah nodded. 'Thanks.'

'You too?' Tom asked John.

'Yeah, thanks,' replied John. 'It's been a long couple of days.'

'Come with me,' offered Tom, wheeling back out of the office and across the workshop. Hidden away at the rear was a grubby bathroom with a toilet, sink and shower. It was a small square cubicle, the old mouldy curtain almost falling off, but it would do.

'Hold on a minute,' said Tom. He wheeled off, coming back a moment later with two blue towels, which he tossed to them.

Sarah thanked him and headed off into the bathroom, shutting the door behind her. 'I'll be back,' said Tom, wheeling off to his office to make some phone calls. John stood guard in front of the door, watching the mechanics slowly fixing the cars.

Ten minutes later, Sarah emerged, rubbing her wet hair with the towel. 'Your turn.'

They swapped, Sarah standing outside while John entered the bathroom to take his shower. The water was lukewarm and without much pressure, but it still felt good. It hadn't even been twenty-four hours since Watts and Brand had come into his life and turned it upside down, but it had been a stressful time and he felt better for washing the sweat and grime from his skin.

When he emerged, Sarah was standing halfway across the workshop, talking to Tom and slipping something into her handbag. He wandered over to her as Tom wheeled himself back into his office. 'Got everything you need?' he asked her.

She shook her head. 'Not yet. Some of it may take a little while.' She looked around. 'Let's take a walk.'

John followed her to the rear of the workshop where they found a small back door. It opened into a small path, running between the buildings of the estate and a small river. At the sides of the path, bushes and brambles grew wild. The wind was blowing strongly, cold in his wet hair, but he didn't really mind. Sarah turned left, setting off along the path, and John joined her, walking by her side.

'So, how long ago did you know Tom?' he asked.

'It was about ten years ago, before I was recruited by MI6. We were both independent contractors back then.'

'Mercenaries?'

'Potato, potahto,' she replied. 'We were sometimes brought in to bulk up the numbers, sometimes to do the work that couldn't be officially sanctioned.'

'What...? Black-bag operations, off-the-books wet-work?'

'You don't need to be quite so melodramatic. But basically, yes. We worked for a PMC – a Private Military Company – and we saw action together in Sarajevo, South Africa, Iraq... and a few others, until he was shot in the spine and paralysed from the waist down. That's when I decided it was time to get out before I got my own bullet.'

John stopped, shaking his head slowly. 'Sometimes I think I really don't know you at all any more.'

Sarah turned to face him. 'As I said before, John, there are some things in my life that I'm not particularly proud of. Some things that if I had to do it all again, I might do differently. But my time with you isn't one of them. Deep down inside, I'm still the Sarah you knew back then.' She took his hand in hers and started walking again, pulling him along. 'If there's anything you need to ask me, you can.'

John thought for a moment as they strolled together in silence. 'Did you miss me?' he eventually asked. 'After we split up?'

A small wry smile appeared on her face as if she was remembering a pleasant far-off memory. 'To be honest… not initially. You weren't the only one who could be a jerk back then – I could be a heartless bitch at times, as I'm sure you can remember. But as time went on, and I had one failed relationship after another… yes, yes I did. Our time together wasn't perfect, but I'll always remember it with fondness. You don't know what you've got until it's gone, as they say.'

Silence descended again, and they continued to walk along the path hand in hand. A few minutes later he spoke up again. 'How many people have you killed?' he asked her.

She sighed. 'Too many. I'm not proud of it, and I've never taken pleasure in it. But in my line of work… sometimes it's a necessary evil.'

They came to a bench and sat down, looking out over the river. There was a family of ducks slowly paddling their way across the water. Sarah kept hold of his hand, holding it tight. 'It can make it hard to sleep sometimes, seeing the faces of the people you've killed in your mind, especially the first few times. But you have to focus on why you did it. The people you saved. The hostages you rescued. The women and children who are alive because of what you did.'

Sarah turned to face him, and John thought he could see a hint of a tear in her eye. 'I may be a killer, but I'm not a *heartless* killer. You have to believe me.'

'I do,' whispered John quietly.

'After I quit the PMC, I was ready to give it all up for good, go back to a life of normality. Maybe even try and find a husband and settle down, do the whole two-kids-and-a-dog thing. That's when I was approached by Henry Sandford; he was the man who became my handler at MI6. He convinced me that I could use my skills for good, to help improve the world for all of us.'

'And now he's dead.'

'Yep. He was a good man. He had a wife and kids. He was never meant to be on the front-line of anything.'

'I'm sorry,' said John

'Why? It wasn't *your* fault.'

'No, but still…'

'It's *my* fault, John. I can't have taken enough care. Maybe if I'd been better at my job, maybe if I'd gotten the smart-card to him sooner…'

'You can't blame yourself.'

'I *can*. I know I shouldn't do, but there are still times when I do.' She sighed, her head dropping slightly.

John let go of her hand, instead putting his arm around her shoulder.

'When this is over, that's it,' she muttered. 'I'm out. I've had enough of this shit.'

She stood up and held out her hand to John. 'Walk with me,' she said with a smile. 'Let's just walk a while in silence.'

They returned to the garage a few hours later as the sun was setting. The van was now sitting in a different spot out front. Its front and side panels were still crumpled and dented, although not nearly as badly as before. In addition, new front lights, wing mirrors and a number plate had been installed. Large rental company decals had been added to the sides and rear, giving it an extra level of authenticity and anonymity.

As John admired the handwork, Tom came rolling out of the workshop. 'We did the best we could at short notice,' he said. 'But I think it looks pretty good.'

Sarah gave him a nod of agreement. 'Not bad. And the other items?'

'The ammo will be here first thing in the morning. Not sure about the silencer yet – I'm still waiting for a call back.'

'Have you got anywhere where we can hole up until then?' she asked, flashing him a smile. 'We're trying to keep a low profile.'

'There's an old portacabin of ours round the side of the workshop. It's got a heater, a small TV, a kettle. It's not quite the Ritz…'

'It'll do,' said Sarah with a smile.

'I'll get you the keys,' said Tom. He started to wheel off when he stopped. 'Do you need any food?' he added. 'I can send one of the boys to a drive-through for you?'

'That would be grand, thanks,' said Sarah.

John liked the sound of a warm meal and a roof over his head for the night – even if it was just burgers and thin asphalt roofing.

Tom rolled away again, coming back a couple of minutes later with a single key on a keyring. 'We'll be shutting up shop shortly. You sure you'll be okay?'

'We'll be fine,' smiled Sarah.

'You're not expecting anyone to track you down here are you? I could do without any undue attention to my business.'

Sarah shook her head. 'I think we'll be fine for tonight.'

Tom pulled out another set of keys from his pocket. 'Here are the keys for your van. One of the boys will be round in a few minutes with some food.'

Sarah and John thanked him and then returned to their van where they unloaded the sleeping bag and blankets, as well as Sarah's backpack full of her possessions. They only had to wait a few minutes for their food to be delivered. The mechanic hadn't known quite what to get so had been busy. The brown paper bag was full of burgers and fries, chicken nuggets and doughnuts. In addition, he had brought hot coffee, hot chocolate and soft drinks. John thanked him profusely, and then they headed for the portacabin.

The inside of the small cabin was cramped, a desk and various filing cabinets taking up much of the space. The desk had a small television sitting on it and a well-worn leather office chair behind it. A low coffee table near the door held a kettle and several mugs as well as a small portable heater. It was cold in there, but with the heater on it slowly started to become hospitable. They both sat on the floor by the filing cabinets, silently watching TV while they ate their food.

'Do you have a plan?' asked John, when they had both had their fill.

'For tonight? I've got a few ideas.'

'No,' said John with a shake of his head. 'For getting the smart-card back.'

'Maybe. I need to sleep on it.'

'Care to share?'

'Not just yet. I need to work things out in my head.' She got up, spreading the sleeping bag and blankets out on the floor next to them. 'We ought to get an early night though,' she suggested. 'It might be a long day tomorrow.'

She stared undressing, stripping down to her underwear before slipping under the blankets.

'Are you going to join me?' she whispered seductively.

John came over and kneeled down next to her. He looked into her eyes and they could both detect a sense of longing in the other. However, John simply reached over and took hold of one of the blankets, picking it up as he got back to his feet. He turned so he didn't have to look at her.

'I'll take the chair,' he sighed wistfully.

Chapter 10

There were no blinds or curtains on any of the windows and they were both woken early by the sunlight streaming into the cabin. It was a clear day, the sky bright and blue, but also bitterly cold.

They got dressed, eating the cold leftovers of the previous night for breakfast. A short while later Sarah spied Tom arriving to unlock the workshop and she went out to meet him, leaving John alone in the cabin to finish his cold and stale burger.

He watched her silently through the window as she wandered over to Tom. They appeared to talk for a couple of minutes before he passed her two small packages wrapped in plain brown paper; she slipped them nonchalantly into her bag. She returned a few minutes later, letting herself back into the portacabin.

'Have you got everything you need now?' asked John.

'Yep, John came through for me. I've got the ammo, the silencer and some cash,' she said. 'We need to get going, just as soon as we've packed.'

'So you have a plan then?' he asked her.

'I think so.'

'So what is it?'

Sarah swallowed. 'We need to find him,' she said. 'The man who has your wallet.'

'Watts,' John told her. 'He called himself Watts. And I don't know if he's alone or not. I only met two of them, him and his partner, Brand, but there might be more.'

'We've just got to hope there were only the two of them. But the longer we wait, the more chance there is of him getting some backup. We need to find him, and we need to do it quickly.'

'And just how do you propose we do that?' asked John. 'We went back to where they took me; there was nothing there.'

'I have an idea,' sighed Sarah, 'but you're not going to like it.'

'Try me,' said John.

'You need to call your wife and ask her to meet you.'

'But… you said that was a terrible idea. You said they'd be listening in on her calls.'

'I'm counting on it.'

'But…'

'If you arrange to meet her, then we can draw him out. We can ambush him… I can take him.'

'You can't be serious?'

'Can you think of a better way?' she asked.

'I'm not going to gamble with my wife's life, Sarah.'

'Your wife's life is already in danger, John, as is your daughter's.'

'Last night you said I could protect her by *not* calling her.'

'That was then, John. This is now. Staying away from her is only going to keep her safe for so long. They'll eventually go after her if they can't find you. At least this way, we get to do it on our terms.'

John flopped down in the office chair. 'I must be mad listening to you.'

Sarah stepped closer. 'I know this isn't ideal. But honestly… it's the best chance we have. That *you* have.'

John closed his eyes and sighed. 'So what do you suggest?'

'You make the call. Tell her you need to see her, that you've got something you need her to keep safe. *That* will get their attention if they're listening.'

'And if they're not?'

'If they're not, then you get to tell your wife to get to safety... to get into hiding until this is all over. We'll just have to come up with another plan to track them down.'

John thought for a moment. 'How did you track *me* down? When they took me?'

Sarah smiled and raised an eyebrow flirtatiously. 'Tricks of the trade, John.'

'And that won't work here?'

She shook her head and frowned.

'So this is the only way?'

This time, a nod and a smile.

'I must be mad,' he muttered again.

Half an hour later, John was standing in a phone box in the street outside a quiet country pub. He was amazed they could still find one. He thought they'd all been removed, but apparently there were still a few left, probably due to the shocking state of mobile reception in remote places like this. He took a final look around to make sure no one was watching and then picked up the handset, inserting some coins and dialling his home number. There was an agonizing ten seconds as the phone rang, and then it was picked up.

'Hello?' It was Amy. She sounded scared and nervous and John couldn't blame her. Just hearing her voice lent him a degree of calmness though; she was an island of sanity in the sea of madness in which he was now afloat.

'Amy. It's John.'

'*John*! Where the fuck are you? Are you all right? I've been worried to death.'

'I'm okay,' said John. 'It's a long story and I can tell you everything, but not over the phone.'

'What the fuck's going on, John?'

'It's complicated. Like I said, I need to see you. There's something I need to give to you, for you to keep safe for me.'

'Well, why don't you just come home and give it to me?'

'I can't, Amy. It's not safe.'

'Not safe? What do you mean, John?' Her voice was full of frustration.

'Amy... if you love me at all, you have to trust me. Do you trust me, Amy?'

There was a short pause before she replied. He thought she was probably running through the implications of his question. She was probably fearing the worst, although what she imagined probably wasn't nearly as bad as the truth. 'Of course I do, John,' she said with a resigned sigh.

'Then can you meet me in the town centre in about an hour?' He looked at this watch. 'Call it noon. In the square, by the fountain? You know, near that little café where we had coffee last month?'

'Okay...' said Amy hesitantly. She sounded unsure.

'What about Olivia? Has she been asking about me?'

'She's fine. I told her you had to unexpectedly go away for a couple of days for work. It wouldn't be the first time, but I'm not entirely sure she believes me – she could probably see how worried I was.'

'Can you tell her to go and stay at a friend's house tonight?'

'Sure, I guess so... But why?'

John ignored her question. 'Not her best friend. Tell her just to pick a random friend and go and stay with them for the night.'

'Well… okay…'

'But not a boy,' added John as an afterthought. He had enough to worry about already.

'Why, John? Can't you tell me what's going on?'

John closed his eyes and sighed. 'In an hour,' he said, 'I promise.' He hung up the phone and looked at his hands; they were shaking.

An hour later, John was sitting on the side of the fountain in the town centre. The sun was still shining brightly in the clear blue sky and the square was full of people making the most of the good weather; it was lunchtime and the area was packed with shoppers and workers out on their lunch break.

John's eyes kept darting back and forth, scanning through the crowds as they hurried around, trying to see any trace of Amy. He couldn't see Sarah anywhere, but he knew she was out there somewhere. Or at least he hoped she was, keeping a watchful eye over him in case Watts returned.

He looked at his watch; it was 12:05. She was late. He was full of nervous energy, and he noticed that his left foot was tapping the floor restlessly. He stood up, partially just to do *something*, and partially to get a better view through the crowds.

As he paced up and down in front of the fountain, he glanced at his watch again. It was 12:08. Where the hell was she? Something was wrong.

All kinds of thoughts began to race through his mind. What if she wasn't coming? What if Watts had intercepted her on the way here? He didn't want to think about what a man like that might do to her.

He checked his watch again: 12:10. Where the fuck was she?

Then he spotted her. She was wearing a thick blue coat with the hood up, striding quickly from out of a side street towards him, almost jogging. John set off towards her, closing the distance until they met.

As they neared, John looked at the expression on her face, which was ringed by the hood of her coat. He couldn't tell if she was relieved to see him or mad at him. It could so easily be both.

'Well,' she said bitterly. 'I'm here.'

'It's good to see you,' he replied. 'I'll explain, but not here. We need to go. Where are you parked?'

Amy looked confused and flustered. 'For fuck's sake, John. What's going on?'

John took her by the hand and started to lead her back along the way she had come. For a second she obstinately refused to move, but then she acquiesced, allowing herself to be pulled along.

John stopped as he entered the side street that Amy had emerged from. 'Which way?' he asked as he looked back over his shoulder, checking to see if anyone was following them.

Amy sighed. 'This way,' she said as she took the lead, taking him off down another side street. 'I had trouble parking, that's why I'm late. I'm parked on a meter over here.'

They hurried hand in hand down the street until they spotted their white Audi. Then Amy let go of John's hand, fishing her keys from her handbag and unlocking the car.

John carefully looked both ways, checking for Watts as well as oncoming traffic, and then stepped into the road to get to the passenger side door. As he stood next to the car, he slowly surveyed the street in both directions, scanning all the faces. He was relieved not to see Watts, but also nervous with anticipation. He had expected something by now, but maybe Sarah had already taken care of him.

The passenger window started to open before him. 'Are you coming?' called Amy from within the car as she turned the key and started the engine.

John took one last look back and forth and then opened the door, climbing inside. 'Head straight ahead,' he suggested, pointing down the road. 'Head for the A61 out of town.'

'Okay,' muttered Amy as she indicated and pulled into the stream of traffic, heading along the road at a steady speed. She was silent as she set off, waiting until they were cruising comfortably down the road before she resumed their conversation. 'Are you ready to talk to me yet?' she asked.

'In a minute,' he said. 'Let's just put some distance between us. Take this left,' he added as they came up to a junction.

Amy checked her mirrors and indicated before pulling left onto a smaller road. 'Between us and who, John?' She still didn't understand.

John ignored the question. 'Take this right,' he asked her instead.

She turned right, pulling onto a dual carriageway and picking up speed. A couple of minutes later they pulled back off, taking one road after another, Amy diligently following John's directions.

'Okay,' said John as they pulled off the main road into a quieter street. This road was long and straight, a single wide lane in either direction with parked cars lining both sides. They were approaching a junction. 'Go straight across here,' he said. 'It's not too far now. Then–'

His words were cut short as another car shot out of a side street, swiping the rear of their own. Their car span around, out of control. They glanced off a large truck parked at the side and bounced back into the road, skidding uncontrollably until they smashed sideways into another parked car. The car came to a halt pointing in the correct direction again after having spun three hundred and sixty degrees. The engine had stalled; Amy had frozen with her foot instinctively pressed hard on the brake and had forgotten to press the clutch.

'Are you okay?' asked John breathlessly.

'I... I think so,' she stuttered. Her face was deathly white and her hands were shaking.

John turned to look out the back window. A black BMW was stopped askew across the junction, its front-right side crumpled and bashed. Then he froze as he saw a man climb out of the car, dressed in a dark grey suit; it was Watts.

'Drive!' he barked at Amy.

'What?'

'Go! Just Go!'

'We can't just leave, John,' she cried in disbelief. 'We've been in an accident. We need to exchange insurance details. We need to call the police.'

Watts was striding purposely towards them. He was reaching into his jacket.

'We need to go. *Now!*' he shouted, and then their back window exploded with the crack of a gunshot. 'For fuck's sake Amy,' he cried. 'If you never do another thing I ask of you, will you fucking drive!'

Amy turned the key in the ignition, and John was relieved to hear that the accident hadn't been fatal to their old car. She put it in gear and pressed the accelerator. As they pulled away, there was a screech of plastic scraping against the road and then as the car picked up speed the rear bumper came free, bouncing across the road.

'Faster,' urged John as he looked out through the remains of their rear window. He saw Watts looking at him, carefully aiming for another shot; then a white van shot out of another side road just behind them, screeching to a halt directly between them and him. They could hear the sounds of two more gun shots, then another three.

'Left here,' shouted John as they reached another junction, and Amy threw the car around the corner. It slipped sideways, but she just about managed to keep control, the car fishtailing along the road before she managed to get it steady. In the distance John could hear more gunfire.

'What the fuck, John!' cried Amy between gulps of air. She was crying profusely, tears running down her face and ruining her make-up. She wiped her arm across her face, only making it worse. 'What the hell have you got yourself caught up in?'

John ignored her question. 'Take the left up ahead,' he instructed.

Amy took the turn, too mentally numb to think properly, just following his orders as he gave her directions. Two minutes later they pulled off the road into an abandoned industrial estate – the location where he had agreed to meet up with Sarah.

'Go through that passageway,' directed John, pointing to a gap between two factories. 'There should be a car park behind the building.'

'What is this place?' asked Amy as she slowed the car to a crawl while they passed through the narrow gap between the tall buildings and into a deserted car park. Despite the fact that it was deserted and clearly had not been used for a long time, she still pulled neatly into a parking spot, turning off the engine and putting on the handbrake.

Amy pulled out a handkerchief, wiping her faces and eyes. 'John,' she said, slowly and deliberately. 'Was that man trying to kill us?'

John nodded.

'*Why* was that man trying to kill us?'

John opened the door and stepped out, ignoring her question for the moment. He glanced up and down at the car; it would be an insurance write-off. The front of the car was smashed, most of the lights shattered, and the rear bumper was missing. The entire left side of the car was crumpled, and he imagined the driver's side would be the same. The rear window was in pieces all over the rear seats.

John returned to the narrow passageway they had driven through. He was relieved to see that no one appeared to be following them. Amy was still sitting in the car, her head drooped forwards. He hurried back to her; she was probably in shock.

He opened her door and crouched down next to her. 'I'm sorry,' he said, laying a hand gently on her leg. 'This was never my plan. I never meant for any of this to affect you.'

'For what to affect me, John? Will you *please* tell me what's going on?'

John swallowed. 'It's complicated. It all started about a week ago. It started when...' His voice trailed off as he heard the sound of a vehicle approaching, and he stood up, taking a step back towards the passageway. From behind him, he could sense Amy climbing out of the car after him.

John breathed a sigh of relief as he saw a battered white van pull into the car park, Sarah behind the wheel. She slowed down, pulling to a halt next to them. John could see two bullet holes in the side of the van. The engine turned off and then the door opened, Sarah climbing out to face them.

Amy took a step forwards, her head tilting as she tried to place the face of the woman before her.

John swallowed and took a deep breath. 'Amy, this is Sarah.'

'Sarah?' muttered Amy as she tried again to place her. Then it came to her. '*Your ex?*'

John nodded apologetically.

'You've been with *her* for the last two days?' She was almost hysterical.

'Yes, but it's not what you think,' started John.

Amy stepped forwards and swung her arm. It caught both of them by surprise and the violent slap made Sarah's head snap to the side.

Sarah gave her head a little shake and slowly turned to face Amy again. She gently rubbed her cheek, which was now bright red. 'I'll give you that one for free,' she grumbled bitterly, 'given that I slept with your husband. But if you hit me again, you *will* regret it.'

Amy turned to face John instead. 'Is it true John? Did you sleep with her? Not all those years ago, but recently? Tell me you haven't just spent the last two days shacked up with her?'

'It was just the one time...' he started, figuring that honesty was the best policy, but that was clearly the wrong thing to say. Amy went to slap him too, but as she drew her hand back, Sarah grabbed her arm firmly.

'Now is not the time for petty bickering,' said Sarah slowly and calmly.

'Get your fucking hands off me,' snarled Amy, turning to face her. Sarah slowly released her grip.

'Please, Amy,' sighed John. 'She's here to help us.'

'*Help us*?' spat Amy, almost apoplectic with fury. 'Help us break up, John? Help us to see that she wants you more than me?'

John shook his head and held up his hands, his fingers open and his palms towards her. 'This isn't about us trying to get back together. She's in trouble, Amy, and she needs my help. She's in trouble, I'm in trouble... and now you are too.'

Behind Amy, Sarah had stridden off towards Amy's car and was now looking through the window. She strode round to the back and popped open the trunk.

'Will you please tell me what the fuck is going on, John?' said Amy between gritted teeth. 'Or I swear to God I am going to drive out of here right now and to hell with the both of you.'

'Can you calm down, and listen to me rationally?' asked John, very slowly and calmly. 'Listen to what I have to say, and then if you still want to leave... you'll get no resistance from me.'

Amy closed her eyes and took a deep breath. She was still clearly shaken, her face a mess of tears and make-up, and it looked like she was still shaking. 'Okay,' she muttered.

John took his jacket off, wrapping it around her shoulders and leading her over to a low wall where they could both sit down. Sarah still seemed to be rummaging through their boot. She stood up, removing a small first aid kit.

'A week or so ago, I got back in contact with Sarah,' began John. 'I thought it would be nice to get back in touch. I didn't have any ulterior motives at the time–'

'But...' interjected Amy.

'There was a moment of weakness,' admitted John. 'I underestimated the effect she would have on me, and for that I'm truly sorry.'

'Sorry you got caught,' muttered Amy, but John ignored her.

'It was a mistake, and one I'm going to have to live with. I still love you and want to make this up to you, but when this is all over, whatever decision you want to make, I'll support you.'

'Do you not remember last time, John?' cried Amy between sobs. 'Last time you were with her? It certainly didn't work out well for you. She left you then, and it almost broke you. Do you want to go through that again?, Because I tell you now, John, sooner or later she's going to leave you again, and this time you're not going to have me around to help pick up the pieces.'

'Amy...'

'Do you want to be with her, John? Is that what you want?'

John shook his head. 'I still love you, Amy. I can't deny I still have feelings for her, but you're the one I want.'

'Then what is all of this about, John? Why was someone shooting at you? At us?'

'Sarah is a spy, Amy.'

'A *spy*?' she spat in disbelief.

'I know it sounds crazy, Amy, but you won't believe the couple of days I've had since I last saw you. I was kidnapped and interrogated by two men pretending to be police. Sarah tells me they were probably Russian agents. One of them was going to kill me... until Sarah saved me. She killed him with her bare hands, Amy. The other man... he was the one shooting at us earlier. I... I don't know what's happened to him now.'

'And why has any of this got anything to do with us?'

'They knew that I'd been in contact with her. They wanted what she had, and thought I might know where she was.'

'And what is it that she has, John? What the hell has she got that they want so badly?'

'A smart-card. It's got some kind of top-secret documents on it.'

'And where is this smart-card now?'

'We're not sure. It was in my wallet, but they took that when they kidnapped me. I don't think they know it's in there though. Sarah hid it there after... well, *afterwards*.' He glowed slightly with embarrassment as he said this to his wife.

'So what now, John? What the hell are we supposed to do now?'

'I don't know. We thought they would be watching you and bugging your phone. We thought that if they knew we were meeting, we could draw them out and then Sarah could try and ambush the other spy when he came after us. Judging by her demeanour, I don't think that went to plan.'

'Hold on,' exclaimed Amy. 'Whoa, whoa, whoa.' She stood up, looking down at John. There was fury written across her face. 'You were using me as *bait?*'

'It's not how it sounds,' said John apologetically, although he knew that was the wrong thing to say the moment the words left his lips. It had been *exactly* how it sounded.

'I can see how *she* might come up with a plan like that–' started Amy.

'She isn't trying to hurt you,' John explained quietly.

'Shut the fuck up, John,' spat Amy. 'How am I meant to trust you after this? How can I ever trust another thing you say to me?'

'I'm sorry,' he repeated. 'I was only doing what I thought was best for you.'

'What, when you fucked her?'

'No, no,' said John. He looked down at his feet, unable to look his wife in the face. 'After that. When it was clear how bad a mess we were in. It was the best choice from a bad set of options.'

'What about our daughter, John? What about Olivia?'

'Did you send her to a friend's house, like I asked?'

'Yes.'

'Then hopefully she should be safe for now.'

'*Hopefully?* I swear to God, John, if you've put her life in danger...'

'We need to go.'

John looked up. Sarah was standing behind Amy, her hands on her hips.

Amy turned to face her. 'Why should I do anything you say?'

'Because I'm the only one standing between you and a deadly assassin willing to kill you and everyone you care about. You may not like me,' she added, to which Amy gave a little scoff, 'but compared to him, I'm Mother-fucking-Teresa.'

Amy looked like she was about to explode with rage and then she subsided, her shoulders slumping. 'If what you two say is even half true, I really don't have much choice, do I?'

John looked at her and shook his head slowly. 'Sorry.'

'Come on,' said Sarah. 'I think I gave him the slip, but he'll still be looking for us. We need to put some ground between us while we work out our next plan of action. You two can sort out your marital issues another time.'

Chapter 11

Half an hour later, they were parked in shopping centre car park on the edge of town. John and Sarah had climbed into the back of the van while Amy had remained in the front, blankly staring out through the windscreen.

'So what now?' asked John.

'We need another plan for drawing him out,' explained Sarah.

'So what happened last time? What went wrong?'

Sarah sighed. 'I was trying to keep tabs on you and make sure I didn't lose you, while also keeping a lookout for Watts. I expected him to try and intercept you two near the fountain, but I think he just tailed your wife when she drove there and stayed in his car the entire time, ready to follow the moment you two left together. Luckily I knew where you were going, and managed to catch up with him. At one point I thought I'd managed to distract him enough to let you two get away, but then he gave me the slip. I only just caught up with you in time. Then it all turned to shit, and I only just got away in one piece.'

'Thanks for that,' said John with a weak grin.

'The only trouble is, we've got no way of making contact again now.'

'I'm not sure about that,' replied John. 'Amy?' he called to his wife. She continued to stare out the front of the van. 'Amy,' he called again softly.

Amy shook her head softly. 'I'm sorry,' she muttered. 'Did you say something?'

'Can I borrow your phone?'

Lost in a daze, Amy reached into her handbag and pulled out her phone, handing it across to John.

John held it up between himself and Sarah. 'He may still have my phone. We can call it – see if he answers.'

Sarah nodded. 'We can do that, but how are we going to lure him out a second time?' She thought for a moment. 'We need to propose a trade.'

'You're assuming he hasn't found the smart-card yet.'

'If he had, then he wouldn't still be coming after us,' she said. 'At least, I hope so...'

John supposed that there was always the possibility he already had it and was just trying to clean up any loose ends.

'We've got to offer him the smart-card in exchange for leaving you and your family alone,' she continued. 'It's the only thing that sounds plausible enough. We get him to come somewhere I know, somewhere on our terms. We plan an ambush and we hope for the best.'

John typed Amy's PIN into her phone and went to her contacts, scrolling through until he found his number. He was about to dial the number when Sarah gently took his hand. 'Let me do this,' she offered. 'I've more experience in these situations – I've dealt with people like him before.'

John acquiesced, and she took the phone, hitting the call button. She waited a few seconds, listening to a recorded message, and then put the phone down. 'Your phone's no longer in service,' she said with a sigh.

'The battery's probably flat,' he suggested. He thought for a second. If he's monitoring our phones, presumably we could just call anyone on her phone.'

Sarah shook her head with a grimace. It's unlikely that he's got access to your mobile phones. Your home line is reasonably easy to tap; just open up the junction box, find the right wire and you're in. Mobile phones are much harder; the data is encrypted for starters. If this were GCHQ or MI5 we were talking about then yes, they might be listening to your mobiles – they've got official rules and procedures to give them access for just such a circumstance. But the Russians? It possible they might have a man on the inside, willing to pass them information for a price, but it's unlikely.'

'So what do we do then?'

Sarah thought for a moment and then picked up the phone again. 'Do you have an answering machine?'

'What?'

'At home. Does your home phone have an answering machine?'

'Yes,' replied John. They could call that again, he realized; leave a message, and hope he was listening.

Sarah scrolled through the contacts until she found the entry for John's home phone and clicked on it.

The phone rang six times before it was picked up. 'Hi,' came Amy's cheerful voice. To John, it now sounded like it was recorded an age ago. 'I'm afraid we can't come to the phone right now, so please leave a message after the tone. *Beep.*'

'You know who this is,' stated Sarah, slowly and deliberately. 'I want to propose a trade. The smart-card in exchange for leaving John and his family out of this. This is between you and me, and it's got nothing to do with them.' She gave John a knowing smile as she said this. 'Call me back to discuss where to meet.' She recited Amy's number, and then hung up the phone. 'Nothing to do now but wait.'

They didn't have to wait long. Less than five minutes later, Amy's phone buzzed into life, vibrating its way across the floor of the van. Sarah picked it up, glancing at the screen: *Number withheld.* She answered the call, putting the call on speaker-phone.

'I'm here,' said Sarah.

'Who else is there?' came Watts's voice through the loudspeaker.

'John and his wife,' replied Sarah.

'Good,' said Watts. 'They're going to want to hear what I've got to say.'

'You've got to listen to what I've got to say first,' stated Sarah, slowly and forcefully. 'If you want the smart-card, you've got to agree to our terms.'

'I don't think so,' chuckled Watts. 'I'm the one holding all the cards now.'

Shit, thought John. *What did he know? Did he know that he already had the smart-card?*

'I've got someone who wants to say hello,' chuckled Watts. The line went quiet for a moment, and then they heard a young female voice. 'Mum? Dad?'

John's heart sank. He looked at Amy; she had looked bad before, but now she looked like a ghost, deathly white and pale, all of the colour drained from her face. Even Sarah's head dropped, as she realized the implications.

'Mum? Dad? I'm scared.'

'Just be brave, honey,' cried Amy. 'There's nothing to be afraid of – this will all be over soon,' she added, even though she knew full well that this wasn't true.

'Watts...' started Sarah, but John cut across her.

'Just give her back, Watts,' he pleaded, 'and you can have anything you want. You can have the smart-card, you can have me. Just let her go.'

'Good,' said Watts. 'It sounds like you fully appreciate the situation you're in. Stay by the phone. I'll give you a call shortly to discuss *my* terms.'

And with that, the line went dead.

Chapter 12

'What do we do?' cried Amy.

'Let me make one thing absolutely clear,' stated John, slowly and deliberately. 'We're not doing anything to jeopardize the life of my daughter. Or my wife,' he added, then immediately regretted it. It sounded like a total afterthought.

'What, any more than you already have done?' spat Amy, wiping away fresh tears. 'If anything happens to her, John, if they hurt her... I swear to God I will never fucking forgive you.'

'Calm down, you two,' said Sarah, earning deadly looks from both of them. 'You can blame each other later. Right now, we have to think clearly and logically about what we're going to do. When he calls back, he's going to want us to move fast, before we have time to plan anything.'

'We have to give him the card,' said John. 'I'm not gambling with my daughter's life.'

'Too fucking right,' agreed Amy. 'That's the first sensible thing I've heard you say.'

'Once we've got Olivia back, you can do whatever you want,' added John. 'But not until she's safe.'

Sarah gave a resigned sigh. 'You don't understand what's on that card.'

'No,' replied John, 'but you don't know either, unless you've been holding out on me.'

Sarah shook her head. 'Not the specifics, but I do know that it's important – important enough to kill for. People have already died on both sides trying to get hold of it.'

'And our daughter isn't going to be the next victim,' added John.

'I don't care what's on the card,' said Amy. 'I just need our daughter to be safe.'

Sarah sighed a deep sigh. 'Okay,' she said. 'We'll do the swap, the card for your daughter. But when she's safe, I need your help, John.'

'For what?'

'I can't leave that card in their hands – the information is too valuable. Somehow, I'll need to get it back. If we can't, then we need to make sure they can't get to a matching card reader. Destroy them all if we have to, so they can never use the information.'

'But then we won't have the information either.'

'Better no one than them. Promise me, John. Promise me that when Olivia is safe you'll help me.'

'Why me?'

'I've got no one else. I'm on my own here, John.' She looked him dead in the eyes, and leaned closer, close enough so that when she whispered, only John could hear it. 'I'm on my own, and I'm scared. I *need* you.'

She leant back again, her voice returning to its normal level. 'So what is it, John? Are you in or out? What do you say? You and me against the world...'

John looked across at Amy. She exhaled sharply with a brief shake of her head. 'She can fucking have you, John. You can do what you damn well want. You already have.'

'I want *you*,' he pleaded. 'I always have. This has all just been one big mistake. I can make it up to you.'

Amy just shook her head, her eyes turned downwards, unable to look at him.

John turned back to Sarah with a resigned sigh. 'I guess I'm in.'

Amy's phone rang two minutes later. John snatched at it, but Sarah beat him to it, calmly picking it up and accepting the call. She put it on speaker-phone again and then placed it back on the floor of the van between them all.

'Talk to us,' she said.

'Have you got the card?'

'We'll give it to you on one condition... Two actually.'

'You're in no position to make any conditions,' said Watts grimly.

'One,' continued Sarah, ignoring him. 'The girl is free to go after this, as is the wife.'

'If you give me the smart-card, I'll have no need of either of them any more.'

'And two, you bring John's wallet, keys and phone with you.'

'Why?'

'We're just cleaning up. We don't want any evidence of his involvement left behind.'

Watts thought for a second. 'Okay. That's acceptable.' After a brief pause, he added 'You know the abandoned gas works, just east of the city?'

Sarah thought for a moment and then nodded slowly to herself. 'Yes. I do.'

'At the rear of the grounds is an old warehouse. Meet me there in thirty minutes. Come alone and no surprises.'

'It'll be tight, but I think we can make it.'

'For the sake of their daughter, you'd better.'

Twenty-eight minutes later, Sarah pulled the van off the deserted road and into the old gas works complex. The two chain-link gates that used to stand padlocked preventing access to the site were lying flat on the floor and she drove over them at speed, heading straight for the rear of the grounds. In front of them they could see a large warehouse, its two huge front doors standing open.

Sarah drove the van straight towards it. As they drew closer, they could see shapes inside, the interior dim apart from whatever daylight was coming in through the grimy windows. The warehouse was huge, the interior mostly empty, but standing a hundred feet from the entrance they could now see a single car, another black BMW with tinted windows. It was presumably a new one – either that or someone had a good team of mechanics on standby.

Sarah drove in through the open doors and pulled the van to a halt fifty feet in front of the BMW, killing the engine. She looked out through the windscreen, first to either side, then up to the roof. 'I don't like it,' she muttered.

'What's wrong?'

'You couldn't hope for a better place for an ambush,' she said with a sigh. 'There could so easily be men positioned either side of us behind the machinery, men up on the gangways by the roof. If there were a couple of snipers up there, none of us would get out alive. We'd be easy pickings in the crossfire.'

'I don't care,' said John. 'We don't have a lot of choice, do we?'

Sarah picked up her handbag, opening it gently and taking hold of her gun.

'No,' ordered John. 'Leave it. They don't want any surprises, and I don't want any misunderstandings.'

'John,' she said. 'We're here for your daughter, but once we have her… if there's any chance of getting that card, I'm taking it.'

'It's too risky, Sarah. I can't let you risk my daughter's life.'

Sarah shook her head. 'This is already risky. They could very well shoot all four of us as soon as they have the card. We can't trust them, John. We need to take them out before they take us out.'

'*No, Sarah*,' repeated John. 'We have to trust them. I can't risk my daughter's life.'

He reached for the door handle and Sarah grabbed his arm. 'What are you doing?'

'I'm going to get my daughter back.'

'You can't John! You don't know what you're doing.'

'I know enough. You stay here and cover me.' He turned to face Amy in the back of the van. 'Whatever happens, just stay here and keep your head down. I've got enough to worry about with Olivia. I don't want to have to worry about you as well.'

He went to open the door and this time Sarah didn't try to stop him. 'You've got it? You know what to do?' she asked.

'I think so.'

'Then for God's sake, John, just be careful.'

John climbed out of the van, leaving the door open, and started to walk slowly towards the car.

The BMW's headlights came on, the full beams dazzling him, and he put up his arms to shield his eyes. The driver's door opened and a man climbed out, pistol in hand. John could only make out his silhouette as he went to the rear door, opening it and pulling out someone from within. She had a cloth bag over her head, but John thought he recognized the thin feminine figure.

The man placed the barrel of the gun under the side of her ribs and marched her forwards until he and John were about twenty feet apart. John could now clearly see that it was Watts, just as he had expected.

John slowly shuffled forwards, his hands held out before him. As he walked he looked slowly around, scanning their surroundings. He thought he could see movement high up near the roof on either side. He assumed that Sarah knew what she was talking about and there were probably snipers up there.

He stopped five feet in front of Watts and Olivia. 'Are you okay?' he called softly to his daughter. 'Have they hurt you?' He couldn't see any obvious signs of physical trauma.

Olivia sobbed quietly under the hood. 'I'm okay,' she whimpered quietly.

'Smart-card,' ordered Watts.

'I need my stuff first,' John stated slowly and clearly.

'You can have those – and your daughter – when I have the smart-card.'

'I need my wallet and phone first,' replied John keeping his voice flat and level, not taking his eyes from Watts. 'You'll see why.'

Watts frowned and stood still for a moment. Then he reached into his jacket pocket, extracting John's wallet, keys and phone. 'Don't get any funny ideas,' he said, looking him straight in the eyes. 'There are men with their gun sights on you right now, and they won't hesitate to kill either you or your daughter if required.'

'I understand,' replied John calmly, holding out his hand.

Watts took a step forwards, placing the items in John's hand before stepping back again.

John slipped his phone and keys into his trouser pockets and then opened his wallet. He took out the credit cards and the cash, slipping them into his jacket pocket. Then he leafed through the rest of the items, old scraps of paper and receipts that he casually dropped to the floor, and a battered photo of his wife holding a newborn baby in her arms – Olivia when she had just been born. He slipped that into his pocket with the money. He made an elaborate show of checking the rest of it, and then held it out, offering it back to Watts.

'What?' asked Watts, confused as to what exactly was expected of him.

'Take it,' said John. 'You'll see.'

Watts gave him a curious glance, and then stepped forwards, snatching it from him.

'Look inside,' instructed John.

Watts opened the wallet. Inside was a single item; a black card, the size of a credit card, with a small chip in the centre. John could just make out a string of numbers printed across the bottom. *Ty che, blyad?*' he muttered in Russian, his English accent temporarily in hiding.

'It's been in there the whole time,' said John. Despite everything, he had to suppress a smile.

Watts shook his head. He took a step back, placing the gun barrel into the middle of Olivia's back. For a moment John's heart was in his mouth, but then Watts just pushed her forwards. 'Go,' he snarled. 'Go join your father.'

She stumbled forwards, and into John's open arms. He ripped the bag from her head and looked at her. Her eyes were puffy from crying, and her mascara was smeared, but she looked okay. It didn't look like they had harmed her.

'Go,' he shouted to John. 'Get out of here, all of you. And if I ever see any of you piss-ants ever again, I'll shoot you on the spot.' With that, he turned, climbing back into his car.

John pulled Olivia close, hugging her and kissing her gently on her forehead. 'Let's get out of here,' he whispered to her. He looked down at her hands where they were tied behind her back. It looked like a complicated knot of tough rope. It would have to wait.

He put an arm around her shoulder and ushered her back to the van. Amy was waiting at the rear doors, and scooped her up into her arms as she arrived. John helped Olivia climb in, and then jumped up into the van after her.

'There should be a knife in my backpack,' said Sarah.

John pulled the bag open, rummaging within until he pulled out a six-inch combat knife in a sheath. He pulled the knife free and handed it to Amy, handle first. 'Cut her hands free,' he asked her, 'but be careful – it's sharp.'

Amy gave him a scathing look. 'No shit,' she said as she started on the rope.

John looked back at Sarah. She had started the van, but was sitting there with her handbag on her lap. Her hand was slipped inside and John knew that she would be holding the pistol in her hand. 'What did you see?' she asked. 'Who's out there?'

'I think you were right – about the snipers. I could see movement from up near the roof.'

'Fuck.' She peered out of the front window. She too could see movement. 'Fuck, fuck, fuck,' she muttered under her breath. She withdrew her hand from the bag and John was relieved to see that it was empty.

'We need to get out of here, Sarah.'

'I need that card, John.' She sounded desperate.

John looked her in the eye. 'If you go out there with a gun they'll kill you, Sarah, and then they'll kill the rest of us too. It's time for plan B.'

'God damn it,' she muttered to herself. She took one final look out of the windscreen as Watts' BMW backed away from them, and then sighed as she put the van into reverse, retreating slowly out of the warehouse.

'It went okay?' she asked him once they had reached the outside and turned around. She was keeping a watchful eye on the warehouse in the rear-view mirrors.

'I think so,' he said. 'Let's get the hell out of here. I don't think he noticed a thing.'

Chapter 13

Before the exchange, Sarah had told John that when he had been abducted she had tracked him down via a microtransmitter she had hidden on him. After their first night together, when she had hidden the smart-card in his wallet, she had needed some way of finding him again if she survived.

She had noticed that his shoes looked old and sturdy, well worn, like they were used every day. She had inserted a tiny microtransmitter into the side of one heel; it was no bigger than a pin. It was very low power, only able to be detected when it was out in the open, and only with very rough co-ordinates, but it was enough to be able to track him down when he had been abducted, at least to his general location. It had meant that Sarah had needed to keep an eye on the whole area around where he had last been seen, but to her relief it had worked; she had eventually seen him being re-moved from the safe house by Brand and driven away in the back of his car.

Now, that same transmitter was stuck in John's wallet. He had kept it pinned into one of his sleeves, and when he had emptied the wallet of its contents, he had surreptitiously stuck it into its lining. They just had to hope that Watts didn't notice it and that he took the wallet with him, occasionally leaving it out in the open.

Sarah hoped she could use it to track down Watts and the smart-card, but first they needed to get John's family to safety. They pulled the van into a supermarket car park, and Sarah cruised up to the ATM, double parking in front of the cars parked opposite it. John climbed out, and strode purposefully over to the machine. One by one, he went through each of his and his wife's cards, withdrawing the maximum amount of cash he could on each. Then he returned to his wife and daughter.

'Take this,' he said, stuffing most of the money into Amy's hands. 'Get a taxi to the train station, then get on a train. It doesn't matter where, just pick somewhere random. You two need to hide up for a couple of days. Find a cheap hotel, book in with this cash under a fake name. Don't use your credit cards, don't use your phone. In fact, just turn your phones off.'

'Have you met our daughter?' asked Amy sarcastically. 'Do you really thing she can cope for two days without her phone?'

'I don't care,' said John. 'She has to. I'm not kidding, Amy.'

Amy nodded solemnly. 'I know.'

'Just keep out of sight. Two days.' He looked at Sarah, who gave a little nod. 'In two days, this should be over, one way or another.'

'Probably less,' muttered Sarah quietly.

He approached his wife to give her a kiss goodbye, but as he came close she pulled back. It was a small gesture, but quite clear to John, and he didn't press the point. Amy turned to help Olivia out of the van and John moved to her instead, giving her a big hug.

'Look after yourself and your mum, okay?'

'I don't really understand what's going on,' she said, casting a glance towards Sarah, 'but please be careful.'

She probably suspects more than I'd like, thought John.

'I will do,' he said, giving her a gentle kiss on the top of her head. 'I'll see you again in a couple of days, I promise.'

John watched them go, walking hand in hand towards the store entrance and then getting into a taxi that had just dropped off a shopper on their weekly trip. He waited until the taxi had pulled out of the car park and was out of sight before climbing back into the van with Sarah. He'd noticed that Amy didn't once look back.

'Well, John. Looks like it's just you and me again,' Sarah said smoothly, a wide grin spread across her face.

They set off south down the M1. Sarah had put a little black box on the dashboard; it looked and acted like a sat-nav, but rather than leading them towards a set destination, its map instead displayed a red flashing dot indicating the last known location of her microtransmitter. It was further down the M1, about an hour ahead of them and only updating its position every minute or so.

'Can't you go any faster?' urged John.

'I'm doing eighty,' explained Sarah. 'This piece-of-shit van won't go much faster, and I really don't want to attract too much attention. If the police see the bullet holes in the side, they may want to ask some awkward questions.'

They followed the dot as it moved further and further south at speed, until it entered central London where its movement slowed. Sarah was making the best progress she could; they were slowly catching up, but they were still over forty minutes behind.

'They've stopped,' she said as they were pulling off the M1 into much slower traffic.

'What?'

'The location of the tracker hasn't changed in the last five minutes.'

'Is it still online?' he asked.

'Yep, still transmitting, just not moving.'

'So they're at their destination?'

'Either that, or they dumped the wallet. Or they found the transmitter. Or they've switched vehicles and left it behind. Or…'

'I get the idea,' he sighed.

Dusk was starting to settle, and rush hour commuters were starting to clog the roads in front of them.

'This is going to take forever,' muttered Sarah.

They pulled into a small side street almost an hour later. They were on the edge of Brixton, the area a mass of residents and shoppers, although this small back road was relatively quiet and empty. Up ahead they could see a black BMW parked at the side of the road, its lights off. Sarah slowly pulled over onto the pavement, halfway up the street towards the BMW. She turned off the engine and killed the lights.

'Can you see anyone inside?' asked John.

Sarah shook her head. 'No.' In the dim twilight and with the tinted windows, it was hard to see if there was anyone in the car. 'Let's go check it out.'

John reached for the door handle, and Sarah grabbed him gently by the arm. 'I don't think this is a trap. They shouldn't be expecting us…'

'Unless they found the tracker,' suggested John.

'Okay. *Hopefully* this isn't a trap. But just be careful, okay?' John nodded and opened the door. As Sarah climbed out, he could see that she was gripping her pistol tight in one hand.

They both edged slowly along the street, keeping a watchful eye all around. Although the two roads at either end of this quiet street were busy with people, this little side street was deserted.

As they reached the car, Sarah slid cautiously along the driver's side. She peered through the window and then pulled on the handle, the door opening with a click. John saw her lean inside, and then a moment later she was out again. She was holding two things in her hands: a car key with a BMW fob, and his wallet.

'They've abandoned the car,' she stated simply.

'How can you tell?'

'They left it unlocked with the keys in the ignition – it's the easiest way to dispose of a car in an area like this. Torching it would attract too much attention, but leave it unlocked overnight around here? By the morning it will either be in a thousand pieces being sold for scrap, or on its way overseas.'

'And the wallet?'

'Left on the passenger seat. Empty.'

She threw it to him and he caught it. He didn't like having his pockets full of loose notes and cards and he pulled them out, stuffing them back into the wallet. As he was about to slip it back into his pocket he looked at it again and saw the small transmitter still sticking out of it. He pulled it out and handed it over to Sarah. She took it and dropped it into her handbag without saying a word; she looked distracted.

John looked around at the street in which they stood. 'So where are they now?'

Sarah shrugged. 'I don't know.'

John nodded in agreement. 'An hour from here could get you to most of central London. There are a million places they could be.'

'But only one place they *will* be.'

'What?'

'Come with me,' she muttered. She started off towards the end of the lane, and John followed her. As she reached the end she stopped, surveying the busy street ahead.

'Damn,' she said through gritted teeth. 'I know exactly why they came here.'

'Care to share?'

'In a minute. How much money do you have?'

John thought back to all the notes he had stuffed into his wallet. 'About three hundred pounds, I think. Do you need me to check?'

She waved away his offer. 'No, that ought to be enough.' She marched back down the street towards the car and her van. 'If they don't want the car, we'll take it,' she said, using the fob on the key ring to lock it and set the alarm. 'It'll make a nice upgrade from that shitty van.'

'What about its practicality? What about its anonymity?'

'I've decided it's over-valued. I could do with an upgrade.' She dropped the keys into her handbag before opening the back door of the van and climbing inside, where she picked up her backpack. 'I need to change quickly,' she added.

'What about me?'

Sarah gave him a quick glance up and down. 'You'll be fine.' First she took off her jacket, leaving herself in just a white shirt, and then she took off her shoes and skirt. 'No need to get all modest now,' she tutted as John turned around, averting his eyes. 'You got a good enough look the other night.'

She reached deep inside her backpack, pulling out a small black leather mini-skirt which she pulled up over her hips. Then she retrieved a pair of black high-heels that she slipped onto her feet. Finally, she pulled a small make-up bag from the very bottom of the bag, applying some bright-red lip-stick and mascara, as well as a liberal dousing of perfume.

'All done,' she said, as she stuffed her old clothes inside the backpack. 'Oh no, wait…'

She unbuttoned her shirt halfway down her chest, revealing her ample cleavage. Using a compact make-up mirror, she checked herself out. 'No tights or suspenders,' she said with a grimace, 'But I suppose it'll do.'

She threw the backpack to John who caught it. 'Put that on.'

'Where exactly are we going?' he asked as he put his arms through the straps. This thing was heavy.

'We're going to book ourselves into a hotel,' she explained. 'There's one just across the street.'

She climbed carefully out of the van, waiting for John to join her before she locked it. Then she held out a hand for John. 'Let's go.'

'And why exactly do you need to look like that?' asked John.

'I'm hiding in plain sight,' explained Sarah. We need a hotel room for the night. In central London. Paying in cash, without any ID. If we just stroll up, pretending to be tourists or a husband and wife it might look suspicious.'

John understood. 'But a man with an escort... That would easily explain the desire for anonymity.'

Sarah nodded. 'The receptionists here, they've seen it all before. They may judge you inwardly… but they're not going to say anything.'

'Shouldn't we do something about finding Watts and the smart-card first?'

'We can't do anything until the morning. I'll explain when we're in our room. I'm freezing my tits off out here. Literally.'

Chapter 14

John could feel the stares of the other hotel residents as he stood in the hotel foyer waiting to check in. Sarah stood a little way back from the reception desk, giving him flirty glances every time he looked towards her, checking her watch. She was playing the role of someone who wasn't very good at being discreet; she did it well.

'I'd like a double room for the night, please,' said John as he reached the front of the queue. 'Just something basic, as long as it's got en suite.'

'Our standard room is one hundred and fifty pounds a night, breakfast not included,' replied the desk clerk. His eyes were flicking between John and Sarah.

'That will be fine,' said John. He pulled out his wallet and extracted the correct amount, sliding it across the counter.

The clerk opened the cash register, sliding the notes inside. 'And your name?'

'Mr and Mrs Johnson.'

The clerk looked up from his computer at Sarah, standing across the room in her heels and mini-skirt. 'And could I see some ID for you and your wife?'

'I'm afraid we left our ID in the car. Could we show it to you later?' He pulled another twenty-pound note from his pocket, sliding it across the counter. 'I think I mistakenly underpaid you earlier.'

The clerk took the money without a second glance. 'Very honest of you, sir. Thank you very much.' John noticed that the money found its way into his pocket rather than the till as he typed a note in the computer. 'You can show your ID later when you've retrieved it. I'm sure that will be fine.' He carried on typing into the computer, and a plain white card emerged from a machine next to it. 'This is your door card,' he said to John, slipping it into a rectangular cardboard sleeve. Then he picked up a pen, writing the number *220* on the front of it. 'This is your room number. Would you like a porter to help you with your bag?'

'No thanks,' replied John. 'I think my wife and I will be fine.'

Sarah stepped into the hotel room as John held the door open for her. She strode purposefully across the room and stopped by the window, peering out onto the street outside and leaving John to shut the door behind them.

John put the heavy backpack down in a space by the door and shuffled over to join Sarah. 'Now will you tell me what we're doing here?'

Sarah slipped an arm around his shoulder, turning him ever so slightly to look in a particular direction.

'What do you see over there?' she asked softly.

'Shops and businesses,' he replied.

'And that one over there,' she said, pointing across the street and slightly to the side, 'is Gabriel Private Bank.'

'Okay,' said John, 'and what's so special about that bank?'

'Remember when I said that to access the information on the smartcard you needed a reader?' John nodded. 'There aren't many of them. There's one stored at MI6 headquarters, one at GCHQ. And I've left another one in a safety deposit box in there.'

'And they know that?'

Sarah nodded. 'I didn't think *anyone* knew. I don't know how they found out, but finding their car dumped just around the corner... that's too big a coincidence. They must be hired to get it as well as the card itself. It won't be trivial for them to get to the one I left in there, but it'll be a lot easier to get at than the others.'

'You don't think they've already got it?'

'By the time they got here, the bank would already have shut for the night. I think it's safe until the morning.'

'And you don't think they're capable of breaking in?'

'Capable… maybe. But that place is well guarded and secure. I made sure of that before I left the reader there. Breaking in at night, when it's on full lock-down, would be pretty hard. And if any alarms go off… well, we're right here, ready to pounce.

'So you think… what? They're going to rob the bank in the morning?'

'Maybe, but probably not,' she said with a shake of her head. 'More likely is that they have some other plan. Impersonate me maybe, or more likely just pretend to be police with a warrant to have the box opened.'

'Watts can be quite convincing as a police officer,' John agreed. 'I suppose you have a plan?'

'Not much of one, I'm afraid. The best one so far is just to get in there first, grab the reader and then get out before they spot us.'

'And if that doesn't work?'

Sarah exhaled. 'Then it's likely to get bloody.' She glanced at her watch. 'We've got almost twelve hours to kill. Time to get comfortable and order some room service.'

After they had eaten, John stepped into the bathroom, locking the door behind him. He turned the shower on, turning up the heat and the water pressure. As the room started to fill with steam, he undressed, making a neat pile of clothes on the floor.

He pulled open the shower door and stepped into the spacious cubicle, letting the hot water wash over him. The stress of the last few days started to ebb away, and he could feel himself relaxing.

He had closed his eyes, letting the water wash over his face, when he heard a quiet click from somewhere in the bathroom. 'Sarah?' he called out.

The shower door opened, and John saw Sarah standing before him. She was naked apart from her jewellery, and as she slipped into the shower next to him he could see every inch of her feminine curves. 'I didn't want you to use all the hot water,' she said with a grin.

'I locked the bathroom door,' he stated simply.

'You think that was any impediment?'

'No, but I think it did state a certain intent.'

'It's been a while since I had a decent hot shower,' she sighed, as she started to rub herself down with the soap. 'The one at Tom's was pretty puny – I need a serious clean.'

'Do you have no shame?' he chuckled with a shake of his head.

'Do you want me to do your back for you?' she asked, wrapping her arms around him. She started to gently rub up and down his back with the soap, pressing her body tightly against his.

'I think I could manage on my own,' he said, trying to suppress a moan.

'Personally, I always struggle,' she continued. 'Do you think you could do mine?'

'Sarah,' started John, 'I don't think–'

'–then don't,' she interrupted. She glanced down. 'There's no sense in denying that you're enjoying my presence in here.'

'*Sarah–*'

She looked him straight in the eyes. 'Amy doesn't want you any more, John. I think she made that quite clear. And if there's one thing I've learned over the years, it's that you should always take any chance that you have in your life for happiness.'

She moved in closer, closing her eyes and kissing him softly on the lips. When she opened them again, John thought he could sense a hint of sadness in them and possibly even fear.

'You should live life without regret, John, as if every day was your last. And in our case, that may very well be the case.'

This time, it was he who kissed her. 'No regrets,' he whispered quietly.

Chapter 15

John woke at six the next morning to an odd array of quiet metallic sounds. A small side light next to the bed was turned on, providing dim illumination and allowing him to see Sarah stripping and checking her gun. She was sitting in an armchair next to the low coffee table, dressed only in her underwear.

John pulled himself upright in the bed. Despite last night's shower, he was still feeling sweaty and sticky.

Sarah looked up at him as he sat up. 'Sorry,' she muttered. 'Did I wake you?'

John just shook his head to indicate it wasn't a problem. 'Is your gun okay?'

'Just checking it. It's a habit of mine – something to do when I'm nervous and have time to kill.' She pulled back the curtain a crack, peering out into the street, before turning back to John. 'Sleep okay?'

'Yeah. You?'

'Like a baby.'

John crawled out of bed and stood up, acutely aware that he was naked. 'I don't suppose you have any fresh clothes for me in your backpack?'

Sarah shook her head with a smile. 'Afraid not.'

He stepped into the bathroom and emerged a few moments later wearing just his underwear. He was carrying his clothes from yesterday, and he put his trousers in the trouser press, using the small hotel iron to try and restore some sense of order to his shirt.

'Fancy breakfast?' asked Sarah, who was still sitting by the window. 'I'll call room service.'

John brushed his teeth while Sarah ordered them some food, and then came over to join her, pulling back the curtain to peer out into the street. 'Any sign of anything?'

Sarah shook her head. 'Nothing. All quiet.' She stood up and stepped over to her backpack, pulling out some clothes. 'I think we need something more professional this morning. Not too many hookers have safety deposit boxes in private banks.' John tried his best to ignore her as she slipped into her clothes, instead opting to keep an eye on the bank through the window.

'What time do they open?' asked John as he kept a watchful eye on the pedestrians walking up and down the street.

'Not until nine.'

John glanced at his watch. It would still be several hours until then. 'What do we do now?'

'We rest. We wait. We'll also want to check out well in advance – I don't want to leave anything behind here, and we might need to leave in a hurry.'

John stepped over to the table where he had left his phone charging. Despite telling her to turn off her phone, he had still hoped that Amy might have sent him a message, but there was nothing.

A few minutes later there was a quiet knock on the door. 'Room service,' called a woman's voice.

'Just a moment,' called Sarah. She stepped over to the wardrobe near the door, pulling out a hotel dressing gown and slipping it on over her clothes. It was large, white and fluffy, and there was plenty of room in the pocket for her pistol. 'Just in case!' she mouthed quietly to John, who was hastily removing his trousers from the press and putting them back on. When they were both fully dressed, she stepped over to the door, unlocking and opening it with her free hand while the other held on to the gun in her pocket.

A uniformed woman with impeccably tidy black hair stood in the hallway, carrying a tray laden with food.

'Come in,' said Sarah. She watched closely from the doorway as the woman went over to the table in the corner of the room, placing the tray down gently. She kept her hand on the pistol in her pocket the entire time.

'Tip the woman, will you, dear?' asked Sarah as the woman turned to leave.

'Oh. Of course,' muttered John, reaching into his pocket and removing a grubby five pound note. He handed it across to her, and she accepted gracefully with a smile and a nod. Then she left again, Sarah locking the door behind her.

'What's with the gun?' asked John.

'You can never be too careful,' shrugged Sarah as she walked over to the tray: full English breakfast and coffee for two. She picked up a sausage from one of the plates, taking a large bite. 'It's good,' she said to John with a grin, before taking another bite.

John joined her, taking one of the plates and sitting down on the bed with it. She was right; the food *was* good, as was the coffee. John turned on the TV and they ate in silence, watching the early-morning news.

After they had finished eating, John called reception to ask them to send up a razor, and once it arrived he set about shaving. He locked the bathroom door behind him, and this time Sarah didn't interrupt.

When he came out, Sarah had packed her bag and was standing by the door, holding John's jacket. 'We ought to check out early,' she said, 'before it gets busy. Fewer witnesses to remember us if this all goes tits up.'

Once they had settled up, they returned to the commandeered BMW parked in the small alleyway across the street. The lights flashed as Sarah unlocked it, and she opened the boot, heaving her backpack inside. Then they both climbed inside the car to get out of the cold. John thought it was incredibly risky, but it didn't seem to bother Sarah. She didn't think they'd come back for the car – they'd expect it to be long gone by now – but even if they did, they would see them coming in this long narrow alleyway, and maybe that would be an opportunity to get the smart-card back.

But no one came, and at two minutes to nine it was time to go. Sarah reached out over John's lap, opening the glove compartment and slipping her pistol, ammo and silencer inside.

'You're not taking that with you?' exclaimed John.

'They take security seriously here,' explained Sarah. 'There are metal detectors on the door. We'd never get it inside without it being spotted.'

'And if Watts or his friends are there?'

'Well, at least we'll be on an even footing.'

They reached the front door of the bank just as it was opening. There was a burly security guard standing just inside who held the door open for them as they stepped through. The guard gave a quick glance inside Sarah's handbag as they passed one by one through an airport-style metal detector, neither of them setting it off.

The inside of the bank was small and minimalist, with just a couple of desks and chairs and a single teller's window at the rear; a man on the other side of the glass appeared to be sorting through some paperwork. A closed door to their left read *Private – Employees Only*, and a door to their right read *Vaults and Safety Deposit Boxes. No access without an escort.*

A middle-aged woman with platinum-blond hair was standing in the middle of the foyer, dressed in an impeccably smart pinstriped skirt and jacket. 'Can I help either of you?' she asked as she came over.

'Yes,' replied Sarah. 'My husband and I have a safety deposit box that we'd like to access.'

'Certainly, Ma'am,' said the woman. 'Do you have your key?'

Sarah nodded, reaching into her handbag and pulling out a set of keys. She slipped a metallic key about two inches long from the ring and handed it over to her.

The woman stepped over to a desk, pulling out a chair and sitting down. The desk was bare apart from a computer, but there were two chairs on the opposite side, and John and Sarah sat down facing her.

The woman inspected the key, typing the number that was engraved on it into the computer. 'Can I have your name, please?'

'Lucy Butler,' said Sarah. John looked at her with raised eyebrows but Sarah ignored him.

'Thank you, Mrs Butler,' she said. 'You can call me Jill. Do you have any identification?'

Sarah reached into her handbag again, removing a passport and passing it to her. Jill opened it and looked at the information printed on the pages, comparing it to the data on her screen. Then she glanced at Sarah, comparing her likeness to the passport photo. 'Very good, Mrs Butler,' she said with a polite smile, passing the passport back. She stood up again. 'Will you come with me?'

They stood up and followed Jill over to the door that led to the vaults and safety deposit boxes. She lifted up a card that hung from a lanyard around her neck, swiping it through a keypad before discreetly typing in a code. The door gave a quiet buzz as it unlocked and she pulled it open. 'After you...' she offered.

Sarah took the lead and John followed, stepping through the doorway and then down a narrow spiral staircase. Jill took the rear, closing and securing the door behind them.

The staircase opened into a large room. In a corner to their left sat another security guard behind a desk. Despite the lack of distractions, he looked sharp and alert.

Set into the walls of the room were two large bank vault doors, which stood firmly closed, and a third that stood open. To their right were three small booths, each of which had a curtain pulled to one side.

Jill nodded to the security guard, who gave her a casual and irreverent salute back as she pulled a ring of keys from her pocket. 'I'll just be one moment,' she said, stepping towards the open door. On the other side, John and Sarah could see walls of safety deposit boxes.

John looked at his watch. It was ten past nine. 'This is taking too long,' he whispered to Sarah. 'They could be here any minute.'

'Just be cool,' she whispered back. 'We don't want to arouse any suspicion.'

A moment later, Jill returned carrying a long metal box, six inches wide and two feet long. She stepped into one of the booths, placing it on a small table before she stepped out again. 'If you can just let me know when you're done?'

Sarah nodded, and she and John stepped into the booth, Sarah drawing the curtain behind them.

John looked expectantly at Sarah. She lifted the lid on the box, and then lifted out the contents one by one, placing them on the table. First, there were two bundles of money; one composed of fifty-pound notes and the other hundred-dollar bills.

'Here,' she said, pulling a handful of fifties from the stack. 'Reimbursement for all you've had to stump up for.'

'You don't need to…' he spluttered, but Sarah placed the money in his palm, wrapping her hand around his.

'Just take it, John,' she said. 'You've earned it.'

He sheepishly accepted the money, taking out his wallet and slipping the notes into it.

Next, she removed another British passport, placing it next to the money.

'How many of those do you have, exactly?'

'Enough,' she grinned. 'That one's clean – never been used.'

Finally, she pulled out a small plastic and metal device. It looked like a portable credit card reader that a bar or restaurant might use.

'Is that it?' asked John.

Sarah nodded. 'Just need to insert the card, connect it to a computer, and you're away.' She picked up her handbag, opening it and inserting the reader, money and passport inside.

'Are we good to go?' asked John.

Sarah nodded. She slipped her handbag over her head so that it couldn't just be easily pulled from her shoulder and then closed the lid on the box, drawing back the curtain and passing the empty box to Jill.

'Thank you,' said Jill. 'I'll just be one moment.' She turned, returning to the room from where she had taken the box.

'Come on…' muttered John under his breath, impatient at the delay.

Jill returned a minute later, returning the safety deposit key to Sarah. 'Thank you for your custom, Mrs Butler. If you want to follow me…' She turned and headed back to the steps before slowly ascending them. Sarah followed her at a discreet distance, John taking the rear this time.

When she reached the top of the stairs, she opened the door, which didn't appear to have any form of security from the inside. She stepped through into the foyer, and John and Sarah followed, stopping suddenly as they saw who stood before them.

There was a huge, serious-looking man in a dark grey suit and tie standing in the foyer, showing some papers to another member of the bank's staff. John didn't recognize him, but as he turned to look at them, it was obvious that he recognized Sarah.

He immediately pushed the staff member to the side; she fell backwards, the papers falling to the floor. Reaching down, he slipped one hand into his boot and pulled out a knife. Sarah could tell it was a custom ceramic blade – designed not to set off metal detectors. Slowly, he advanced towards her.

This hadn't gone unnoticed by the security guard standing by the door, and he advanced towards the man, holding out one hand in front of him while drawing a taser in the other.

He didn't even have time to yell out a warning before the man in the suit grabbed him by his outstretched hand, pulling him in towards him. As the guard stumbled closer, the huge man let go of his arm, instead grabbing him by the hair. He yanked his head backwards and then savagely slashed across his throat with the knife. A crimson spray flew through the air and then the man with the knife let go of him. The guard collapsed to the floor; he wasn't moving, a large pool of blood already forming underneath him.

The customers in the bank were panicking now, either screaming and running out of the door in fear or scrambling backwards, away from this madman. John froze in shock, but Sarah was advancing. She snatched a lightweight chair from a desk next to her, swinging it up and around so that its legs pointed at her opponent.

They locked eyes, circling one another. Sarah gave a small thrust forwards with the chair, testing him, and he stepped to the side with a grace and speed that John wouldn't have expected from a man of his size.

'Give it me,' he growled, 'and I might let you live.' She jabbed again with the chair and again he dodged it easily.

She tried a third time, but this time he was too quick. He batted the chair to the side with one hand, and it was ripped from her grasp, clattering to the floor. He slashed at her with the knife he held in the other, and she only just drew back in time, the sharp blade slicing through her jacket but falling short of her skin.

He slashed again with the knife, a fast attack slicing through the air, and Sarah jumped backwards out of the way. Again he attacked, driving her backwards until her back hit the wall.

He was closing in for the kill now. Sarah ripped her handbag from around her neck, the strap snapping where it joined onto the body. She held the leather strap tight in both hands, using it to entangle his arm as he brought the knife down towards her and then she pounced forwards, head-butting him directly on the nose.

He staggered backwards, the knife and handbag both falling to the floor. He looked momentarily confused, his nose a broken bloody mess, but he recovered almost instantly. Sarah tried to follow through with a right hook, but he easily blocked it with his left arm, responding with a powerful punch of his own. It caught her on the jaw and her head snapped to the side. Then he followed through with his left hand, punching her on the other side of the head, and she fell, dropping to the floor.

'Sarah!' cried John, who until this point had been standing motionless while the chaos played out around him. He looked down to where the man's knife now sat, lying on the ground midway between them. He ran towards it and their attacker moved to intercept, momentarily distracted from Sarah.

Before John even got near to the knife, he knew he wasn't going to be fast enough. As he drew close, the man collided with him. John felt the impact and then was forcibly grabbed. Next thing he knew, the man had lifted him up and was throwing him through the air.

He felt the shock as he smashed into the glass front of the bank, the window shattering as he flew through it, landing in a crumpled heap on the pavement. He looked up to see the man reaching down for the knife while Sarah lay on the floor, barely moving. 'Sarah,' he cried again. 'Look out!'

She looked up and saw her attacker. He had retrieved his knife and was now heading back towards her. Then she looked to John, lying out on the street. With one hand she grabbed at her handbag, seizing the broken strap and pulling it towards her. She snatched at the bag as it came close, and John thought she must be going for her gun before remembering that she had left it in the car.

Instead she threw it with all her might, lobbing it across the foyer and out of the smashed window, where it fell onto the pavement next to John. 'Run!' she cried.

John grabbed the bag from the floor, staggering to his knees. Their attacker had turned from Sarah to face John once again. He knew what they must have in the bag.

'Sarah!' cried John again.

'Just fucking run!' she screamed at the top of her voice. 'I'll buy you as much time as I can.'

The man had taken a step towards John, but Sarah clambered from the floor, grabbing at his leg. He turned, kicking at her with his other leg, but she didn't let go. Instead, she reached up, grabbing at his groin and squeezing as hard as she could.

The man howled in pain and fury, swiping at her with his hand. He slapped her hard in the face with the back of his hand and she fell back to the floor once more.

John looked at her through the broken window. He wanted to help her, to save her. He wanted to be her knight in shining armour. But he also knew that this man could snap him like a twig. Their attacker wanted what was in the handbag. If he could lure him away, even momentarily, then maybe Sarah would have a chance for escape.

He picked himself up off the floor and ran.

Chapter 16

His feet slipped on the shattered glass as he started to run along the pavement, desperately scrambling back towards the small alley where they had left the car. He could hear police sirens in the distance, and they were getting closer.

The streets were reasonably quiet at that time of the morning, but the few people that were about jumped out of his way as he sprinted down the road like a madman. He didn't look behind him; it would only slow him down, and if he was caught then they would both be in a world of trouble.

He bounced off the wall as he skidded into the side road where they had left the car, but managed to stay on his feet. As he neared the car he slowed, unzipping the handbag and desperately groping around inside for a set of car keys. He pulled one out, only to realize it was the keys to the van.

Shit, he cursed as he skidded to a halt next to the car. He reached into the bag again and this time came out with a set of keys that had a BMW emblem on them. His fingers were almost shaking too much to press the button on the fob, but he managed, and the doors unlocked with a quiet click and a flash from the indicators.

He wrenched the door open, clambering into the driver's seat. He desperately jabbed the key into the ignition, taking three attempts to get it in. When he looked up he could see a familiar silhouette at the end of the street – the huge bulk of the man who had attacked them.

He turned the key in the ignition, put the gear lever into first gear and floored the accelerator. The rear-wheel-drive car skidded and slipped for a split second until the traction control kicked in and then it shot forwards. The power of the engine took him by surprise, and as it accelerated the car slewed into the large plastic bins at the side of the road, bouncing them away across the alleyway. John kept his foot to the floor, changing to second gear as the car accelerated towards their attacker.

For a second, it looked like he wasn't going to move, and John suddenly wondered whether he had a gun after all. Then, at the last moment he dived to the side and John shot out of the side road. He stamped on the brakes, yanking the steering wheel to one side, and the car skipped sideways, coming to a halt a short distance down the road. He had narrowly missed two cars heading either way down the street, both of which had skidded to a halt, their horns blaring.

John looked in the rear-view mirror to see two other men in dark grey suits helping up his attacker. He was shouting violently at them, pointing towards John. Sarah was nowhere to be seen. Then he saw one of the men reach into their jacket, pulling something out.

John floored the accelerator again as he heard the almighty crack of a gunshot. He ducked instinctively, swerving the car around the stationary traffic. There was a right turn up ahead, and he took it, darting out of the line of sight. He didn't slow though, keeping his foot to the floor and driving as fast as he dared through the narrow London streets.

A pedestrian crossing was coming up, and he pummelled his hands into the steering wheel to sound the horn, barely slowing as pedestrians jumped out of the way. The next set of traffic lights was green and he shot through them, swerving in and out of traffic. There was a bright flash of a speed camera, but he didn't care; this wasn't his car, and at the moment a speeding ticket would be the least of his problems.

Gradually, he let the speed die down as the adrenaline started to wear off. He realized he was gripping the steering wheel like a man hanging over a precipice, and he relaxed. Now he just had to worry about what the hell had happened to Sarah.

He was jerked back to the present as a car smashed into the back of him. He snaked across the road, swerving into oncoming traffic and only just able to move back out of the way in time. In his rear-view mirror, he could see another black BMW, and although the windows were dark, he thought he could see two men in dark suits within.

The car behind accelerated again, but this time John was expecting it. Their car rammed into the rear of his, but he was able to control it better, the car swerving left and right but at least sticking to the correct side of the road.

He put his foot down again, desperate to get away from them. A junction was coming up, and he swerved hard right, cutting across both two lanes of oncoming traffic. The cars braked, flashing their lights and tooting their horns, but John ignored them. His rear-view mirror was still full of the approaching BMW.

John swerved hard left and right through the traffic, desperately trying to lose the pursuing car, but to no avail. He had to get away, or this would all be for nothing. He could still see Sarah lying on the floor of the bank, beaten and bruised. He couldn't let them get away with this.

Fuck it, thought John. *I've been through too much to hold back now.* From the left-hand lane he swerved right, cutting across cars on both sides of the road. He pulled into a side road at speed, a one-way street, which he was now travelling down the wrong way.

The traffic was light, but he was still forced to weave in and out to take avoiding action. He lost one wing mirror in a near head-on collision with an oncoming car that didn't spot him until too late, and then the other one against a parked car as he swerved to avoid another driver.

Every time he risked a glance into the rear-view mirror, the BMW was still there. They had probably been trained for this. The best John had was a couple of track days in his youth. He realized that he wasn't going to get out of this by playing safe.

He skidded the car around another corner, almost losing it as the rear end stepped out. This was a longer, straighter road, the traffic still thankfully light, and he floored the accelerator. The powerful engine responded instantly, and he increased his speed until he was doing seventy. The traffic lights ahead were red, but he didn't even slow, swerving onto the other side of the road to avoid the cars, which were stationary ahead of him as they waited patiently for the lights to change. Still the BMW was right with him.

The road ahead was clear now, but there was another set of red lights coming up. He pressed down gently on the accelerator, increasing his speed to eighty.

The driver of the BMW behind was clearly losing his patience. As they approached the junction, he accelerated towards John's car again. The two cars collided, sending John's car swerving across the lanes. Then, as they both shot through the crossing, an articulated lorry came bearing down from the side road. It narrowly missed John's car as he skidded across the road out of control, but it collided directly into the side of the BMW behind.

The car flew sideways, barrel-rolling down the tarmac for at least a hundred feet, bouncing off parked cars and finally coming to a halt as a tangled mess of glass and metal.

John had stamped on the brakes, the car fishtailing wildly as the traction control and ABS desperately tried to keep control, but it was too much. Both the tyres and John's skill had been pushed past their limit. The car swerved first one way and then the other before veering off to the side and smashing head on into the side of a parked car. John felt the sudden force of deceleration, his seat-belt digging deeply into his chest and the airbag exploding in front of him as everything faded to black.

Chapter 17

John jerked back into consciousness. All around car alarms were sounding, and in the distance he could hear screams. He couldn't have been out for long; hopefully only a few seconds. His head was ringing, his vision blurred, but he scrambled for his seat-belt release. As the pressure of the straps disappeared, he reached forwards for Sarah's handbag, which was still lying in the passenger foot well. He was about to open the door when he remembered what she had put in the glove compartment. He leaned forwards again, his chest aching as he did so, opening it and pulling out the pistol and its accessories. He shoved them into the handbag and then opened the door, climbing out of the car on shaking legs that were only just keeping him upright.

'Are you all right, mate?' called a man standing on the pavement. He was holding a leash, which had a small brown terrier on the end of it. 'Do you need me to call an ambulance?'

John ignored him, instead looking at the wreckage. It was a miracle he was all right.

Thank God for German engineering, he thought to himself. *In the cars of my youth I would have been lucky to have come out of that alive, never mind able to walk away.*

He started to walk. He didn't know where, just away. Away from here, away from the car that had chased him.

'Mate!' called the man on the pavement. 'Hey mate, you need to come back!'

John started to run.

❋ ❋ ❋

He ran blindly, zigzagging from street to street, his heart pounding and his lungs burning, until he could run no more. He bent over by the side of the road, drawing deep breaths of air until his head slowly cleared.

He had no idea where he was. No idea where to go or what to do next. He was on a tiny backstreet, a small alleyway housing the back doors to several businesses. All he had were the possessions in his pockets and the contents of Sarah's handbag; he was still clutching it tight in his hands. It looked out of place, a man carrying a woman's handbag in his hands, so he searched through the bins and rubbish that filled the small street until he found what he was after; a relatively clean bag from a local supermarket. He tipped out its contents, placing the handbag inside instead.

Then he stumbled along to the end of the alley. He needed somewhere to hole up – somewhere to crash, to plan what to do next. Across the street was a pub – open but almost deserted at this time of the day. It would do for now.

He staggered across the road, pushing open the door and stepping inside. The interior was warm and cheery, an open fire blazing away in the fireplace.

A barman was busy wiping down tables, and he looked up as John entered. 'What can I get for you?' he asked.

'Can I have a coffee?' asked John. 'Strong and black.'

The barman nodded. 'Not a problem.'

'What about food?'

'The chef won't be in for an hour or so yet, but I can do you some crisps, peanuts, pork scratchings…'

'A couple of packets of crisps would be good. Any flavour.'

The barman nodded again and headed towards the bar. 'Make yourself comfortable. I'll bring them over in a minute.'

John found himself a quiet table in the back of the bar, and hid himself away in the corner. He pulled Sarah's handbag out of the plastic bag, placing it on the seat next to him, hidden under the table. He opened it and took a look at the contents.

There was the money: both the fifty-pound notes and the hundred-dollar bills. He wouldn't have to worry about cash in the near future.

Next he pulled out the two passports. The first was that of Lucy Butler, the passport she had shown in the bank. Then he opened the second one and examined the contents. The photo was clearly of Sarah, although she was a few years younger with a darker, shorter haircut. The name underneath was Marie Mathews. There were no stamps anywhere in it; it looked unused. He slipped it back into the bag.

He looked up to see the barman approaching. He carried a large mug and two packets of crisps, which he placed on the table in front of John. 'Those okay?' he asked, indicating the crisps; they were Cheese and Onion.

'They'll be fine, thanks,' replied John. He didn't know why he had ordered any food – his heart was still racing and he didn't feel in the least bit hungry. 'Should I pay now?' he asked.

'When you're done is fine,' said the barman. 'I'll keep a tab.'

'Thanks,' said John as the barman turned to leave him again. He returned to the bag. He could see her pistol and its silencer sitting side by side, and he left them there, instead pulling out the card reader. It looked like a portable credit card machine, with a small screen, keypad and place into which a card could be inserted. He turned it over, inspecting it from every angle. There were no manufacturer details, no serial number and no instructions. He slipped it back into the handbag.

There was no clue as to what he should do next. Instead he picked up the coffee, taking a deep sip.

He jumped as his mobile rang, vibrating in his pocket and almost causing him to spill the drink. Nervously, he put down the mug and pulled out the phone. The call was from a number he didn't recognize.

'Hello?' he stuttered as he answered.

'You have something that I want,' came a voice that he recognized; it was Watts. 'If you ever want to see her again, you'd better not have done anything stupid with it.'

'No,' he muttered in a low breath. 'I still have it.'

'Good. Luckily for you, we're willing to do a swap – her for the reader.'

'Is she okay?'

'She's fine. She's been through worse.'

'I want to speak to her.'

'No,' stated Watts curtly.

'If I don't hear her voice, I'm going to assume that she's dead – and if that's the case, you're not getting what you want. I'll make fucking sure of that. I may not be good for much, but I'm pretty sure I could smash that thing into a million pieces if necessary.'

The line went quiet for a moment. 'Stay by the phone. I'll call back in a minute.' Then the line went dead.

Two minutes later the phone rang and John frantically took the call. 'Sarah,' he called.

'John,' came her voice and his heart fluttered.

'Are you okay?'

'Don't give it to them, John,' she screamed. 'Don't–'

She had been cut off.

'Sarah!' he hissed in a frantic whisper.

Watts came back on the line. 'Happy now?' He sounded pissed off.

'No, but I'm satisfied that she's alive.'

'Where are you?'

'London.'

'No shit. *Where* in London?'

John sighed. 'I'm not actually sure.'

'For fuck's sake,' muttered Watts under his breath. He thought for a moment. 'Get over to the abandoned Bishops Brewery in the Isle of Dogs. In the centre of the buildings is a courtyard. You've got thirty minutes to get there if you want her to live.' The line went dead.

John swore under his breath as he stood up, picking up the handbag and putting it back in the plastic bag. He hurried over to the bar, where the barman was emptying glasses from a dishwasher and placing them back on a shelf. As John approached, he looked up. 'Do you need something else?'

'No, I just need to pay.'

The barman reached under the desk, pulling out a credit card machine. 'Paying by card?'

John shook his head. He reached into his pocked, pulling out his wallet and extracting one of the fifty-pound notes that Sarah had given him, sliding it across the counter.

The barman picked it up, turning around to the till, where he quickly scanned it with a UV light to check if it was genuine. 'I'll just get your change,' he said once he was satisfied. He pressed a button on the till and the drawer opened with a *ping*.

'Don't worry about it. Keep it,' muttered John. 'I owe you.'

The barman turned around with an expression of surprise on his face, but John was already halfway out the door. He smiled widely and turned back to the bar. 'Now, where did I put that?' he muttered to himself.

Chapter 18

A grey Volkswagen Passat sped across London, John feeding the taxi driver fifty-pound notes every time he had to run a red light.

As the taxi screeched to a halt outside the old Bishops Brewery factory, John checked his watch. He still had three minutes. He leaned forwards from the back seats to speak to the driver. 'You know what to do?'

'Wait here for you.'

'And if I don't come back out?'

'Take the handbag to the address you gave me. Don't you have to go?'

John nodded and slipped him another fifty-pound note. 'Just keep the engine running and be ready to go.'

He climbed out of the cab with the plastic bag, sprinting off towards the main building. As he approached, he could see that the factory and adjoining buildings were set in a rectangle with an open area in the middle, and he headed straight for that. He ran down a passageway between two crumbling bricks walls, and as he emerged he could see a black BMW with tinted windows sitting on the other side of the courtyard, its engine purring smoothly.

The driver's door opened, and Watts climbed out. John stopped. They were about a hundred feet apart.

'Have you brought the reader?' shouted Watts.

John nodded. He kept his arms in the air, the plastic bag held in his right hand. 'Let me see her.'

Watts turned towards the car and nodded. The back door opened and Sarah was pushed out, standing up clumsily. Her face was bloody and bruised, but she was alive.

'Are you okay?' he shouted. She nodded back silently. She looked like she was angry, but John didn't know whether that was because she had been captured or because he had come to make the trade against her direct instruction.

Watts stepped towards her. He drew a gun from under his jacket, placing it up against Sarah's side. 'We want the reader,' he stated loudly.

John took a couple of steps forwards.

'Stop,' cried Watts. 'Show me the reader.'

'It's in the bag,' explained John, slowly shaking the bag in his right hand.

'Take it out. Show me. But take it easy or your girlfriend loses a kidney.'

John slowly crouched down and placed the bag on the floor before reaching inside and retrieving the plastic card reader. He placed it gently on top of the bag, and then stood slowly up, holding his hands up in the air.

Watts grabbed Sarah by the shoulder, pressing the gun into the small of her back. He advanced slowly towards John, pushing Sarah forwards with the pistol. 'Step back,' he ordered and John obliged, taking a couple of steps backwards.

'Further,' said Watts as he drew closer, and John took several steps further backwards, until he was about twenty feet away from the card reader. It was halfway between them now. 'Put your hands behind your head and interlace your fingers.'

John did as he was told, placing his hands on the rear of his head.

Watts advanced, until the card reader was at his feet.

'You have what you want,' said John. 'Now let her go.'

Watts stopped for a second, as if he was considering the request, and then pushed Sarah forwards. 'Here,' he spat with a bitter scowl. 'Have your whore.'

Sarah nervously stepped towards him. 'John,' she muttered, with a tear in her eye. 'I told you not to trade it for me.'

'I don't care,' he said, as Watts crouched down to look at the reader, the aim of his gun never leaving them. 'I just wanted you to hug me one last time.'

Sarah looked at John, who had an odd look in his eyes. She stepped forwards, placing her hands on his hips, moving in so close that he thought she was going to kiss him. 'He won't let us go,' she whispered in his ear. 'He'll kill us regardless.'

'I know,' he whispered back. 'Just hug me one last time. Hug me like you mean it.'

Sarah wrapped her arms around him, and then stopped. John looked her dead in the eyes and gave her a little nod, almost imperceptible.

All of a sudden, she twisted, stepping away from John as she pushed him to the floor. She dived to the floor, rolling as she went, and in her hand she held a pistol, pulled from where John had tucked it into his belt in the small of his back.

Watts fired at them but missed, the bullet flying between the two of them as they both flew to the ground in opposite directions.

Sarah squeezed the trigger from where she lay in the dirt, her shot flying straight and true. The bullet struck Watts in the chest, and he fell backwards, a cloud of crimson spraying out behind him.

John clambered to his knees. 'We need to go.'

Sarah looked towards the BMW. The doors were opening, men with pistols emerging. She started towards Watts, towards the card reader that lay on the floor next to him.

'Leave it!' shouted John. 'It's not the real one.'

'*What?*' cried Sarah.

A gunshot cried out from the BMW, and John and Sarah could feel something *woosh* through the air between them.

'Let's go!' shouted John. He grabbed Sarah's hand and pulled her away, back towards where he had come from. There was another shot, another miss.

Sarah stopped and turned, pointing her gun at the men. She held her breath and fired three rapid shots. One of the car windows exploded, both men diving to the ground. Then she took John's hand and they ran.

They sprinted out through the gates towards the street. 'I trust you have a getaway car,' she cried as they went.

'Kind of,' said John.

She stopped as she saw the car sitting before them. She saw the taxi plates on the front and rear, the livery on the sides, the driver sitting behind the wheel.

'You brought a fucking *taxi*?'

'I lost the car we had and, well, I don't have your talents for acquiring new vehicles.'

Sarah sprinted around to the driver's door, yanking it open.

'Out,' she shouted, pointing the gun at him.

'Whoa, whoa,' exclaimed the driver, putting his hands up. 'Take it easy!'

'*Out!*' she repeated, more forcefully this time.

The driver clambered out, scrambling around to the rear of the car.

John opened the passenger door, picking up Sarah's handbag from where he had left it on the floor. He reached inside and pulled out the bundle of fifties. Then he ran over to where the taxi driver was standing.

'John!' screamed Sarah. 'We need to go. *Now!*'

John slapped the handful of fifties into the man's hands. 'Sorry,' he muttered. 'Buy yourself another car.' He sprinted back to the passenger side of the car, where the door stood open. He could see the black BMW accelerating towards them, plumes of dust rising into the air behind it. 'If I were you, I'd run,' he shouted at the taxi driver as he climbed inside and Sarah accelerated away.

Chapter 19

'Where's the card reader?' asked Sarah, accelerating the Volkswagen as fast as she could down the road. They were on a long wide road, what used to be the main trunk road of the now abandoned business park.

John reached down, picking up her handbag from the floor. 'In here.'

'So what was that back there?'

'Just a normal credit card machine, nicked from a pub.'

'*Fuck*, John. You don't think that was a bit risky?'

'Well, you said I shouldn't trade the real one for you – and I couldn't just leave you with them.'

'I would have been okay.'

'Bullshit, Sarah. They would have killed you.'

'Maybe. I've been in tougher situations.'

'Stop the machismo bullshit, Sarah. I wasn't prepared to let them just torture and kill you.'

Sarah glanced in the rear-view mirror. 'Yeah? Well we're not out of this mess yet.' The black BMW was accelerating towards them fast. 'We're never going to outrun them in this old piece of crap.' She put her hand on the door panel, opening her window.

'John?'

'Yes?'

'Put your seat-belt on.'

John grabbed the seat-belt, yanking it down and snapping it into place.

'Hold on to your seat,' she suggested. The BMW was filling her mirrors now.

She slipped the gears into neutral and grabbed the handbrake, yanking it on and locking the rear wheels. As she did so she yanked the steering wheel hard. The car violently started to spin around and for a moment John thought it was going to roll over. Then she released the handbrake, dabbing at the brakes and spinning the steering wheel in the other direction, correcting their direction perfectly as they ended up pointing the way they had just come. She picked the pistol from her lap, leaning out the open window towards her pursuers and firing three rapid shots into the windscreen before firing again, firing until the magazine was empty.

The BMW slewed across the road, its windscreen a mess of bullet holes and cracked glass, coming to a sudden rapid halt as it collided with a row of bollards at the side of the road.

The Volkswagen veered to the side and then started to spin out of control across the road. Sarah dropped the gun to the floor, seizing hold of the wheel once again, fighting to regain control as she frantically tried to keep the car pointing in the right direction. She stamped on the brakes as the car skidded and span wildly, the ABS desperately trying to maintain traction until it finally stopped, sitting sideways across the road.

'Are you okay?' she asked, her breathing rapid and shallow.

'Yes. Yes, I think so,' replied John. His pulse was racing, his heart in his mouth.

Sarah put the car back in gear, slowly crawling back to where the BMW had crashed. 'We need to check they're dead.'

'And if they're not?'

'They soon will be.'

She drew the car to a halt next to where the BMW had crashed before jumping out, striding over and pulling the driver's door open. A body slumped out of the car. He hadn't been wearing a seat-belt and had smashed into the windscreen, but she guessed that he had been dead before the impact; the back of his head had been blown cleanly off. The passenger had been similarly unencumbered by a seat-belt, and clearly wasn't moving either.

Sarah leant down and opened the driver's jacket, pulling out a gun — a discreet and compact Smith & Wesson automatic. 'He won't need this anymore,' she muttered to John as she checked the cartridge and safety.

'Don't I get one yet?' asked John with a polite smile.

Sarah turned around to face John with the gun in her hand. She held it out to John butt first, but when he reached for it, she pulled it back slightly out of his reach. 'Just remember,' she said seriously. 'Don't shoot at anyone you don't have the intention of killing. Hell, don't even *point* this at anyone you're not intending to kill.' She held it out to him again, and he took hold of it, slipping it into his jacket pocket.

'Please don't shoot either of us by mistake,' she added with a cheeky grin. 'I've left the safety on – for the safety of both of us.' She looked around, surveying the streets around them. 'Let's go,' she said. 'We need to put down some distance and then dump this car. Even with the money you gave him, it still won't be long until the owner reports it stolen.'

'Okay,' he agreed. They started back towards the taxi.

'And for fuck's sake, John. You didn't need to give him all our money – we might still need that. Have you not heard of insurance?'

'Sorry. I wasn't thinking straight. It seemed like the polite thing to do at the time.'

Despite everything, Sarah laughed. 'Poor, sweet John,' she sighed. 'Always trying to do the right thing.'

'Is that not what all this is about?' he said. 'Doing the right thing?'

'Yes,' she replied with a polite smile. 'But sometimes you do have to consider the bigger picture.'

Sarah quickly drove a few miles away and then stopped briefly to remove the number plates from the car. CCTV and automatic number-plate recognition cameras could easily detect a stolen car, she explained, but a missing number plate normally required an actual police officer to do something, and they were far less common.

They then resumed their journey, driving for an hour across London before she pulled over into a small back road. John recognized it instantly. They were back in Brixton, in the street where they had found the Russian's BMW, just around the corner from the bank where Sarah had hidden the card reader.

'Why are we back here?' he wondered aloud.

'The van,' explained Sarah. 'This car's too hot. It'll have been reported stolen, not to mention being involved in a shooting. It's too risky to keep driving it for too long.' John looked out of the windscreen to see the van still parked by the side of the road. 'I wanted to know that it was still here before we ditched this piece of shit.'

She drove for a couple of minutes before she found a suitable spot, swinging the car off the road and down a steep ramp into a tight underground car park. They found an empty space at the far end, and Sarah neatly squeezed the car in the narrow gap.

'Try and wipe your prints off anything you've touched,' she instructed as she pulled a handkerchief from her pocket, wiping down the steering wheel and controls. 'It's not like we haven't left a large trail of evidence behind us… but it never hurts.'

John did the same and then they both climbed out, wiping down the car handles as they did. She picked up her handbag, knotting the end of the strap onto one of the metal hoops to reattach it.

'Can you remember how to get back to the van?' asked John.

'No worries,' said Sarah. 'Just follow me.'

The van had a parking ticket plastered to the windscreen, but thankfully no wheel clamp. Sarah ripped it off, tossing it to the floor. Then she fished the keys from her handbag, unlocking the van and climbing in. She turned to look in the rear and cursed.

'What is it?' asked John.

'My backpack,' she said. 'I left it in the back of the BMW.'

'Oh,' said John. 'Sorry.'

'What happened?'

'I crashed it. Well, I suppose it would be more accurate to say that I was run off the road. I wasn't thinking clearly afterwards. I forgot all about your bag.'

'Never mind,' muttered Sarah, but John could tell she was pissed off.

'At least I remembered your handbag,' he added.

She ignored him, starting the engine and pulling away. 'Let's just drive,' she muttered. She headed north across the city, slowly winding her way through the traffic. After almost an hour she pulled off the road into a su-permarket car park, parking the van in a secluded corner.

She turned off the engine, pulling out the keys and slipping them into her handbag. 'Can you get my phone from out of the glove box?' she asked as she turned to face John.

John pulled the latch to open the compartment and fumbled around inside. He found her phone hidden at the back behind several manuals and packets of sweets. It was turned off, and he passed it over to her. She slipped it into her handbag, not bothering to turn it on, before opening the door and climbing out. John followed her and they left the car park on foot, heading off into the crowds, following the flow of people along the busy streets.

The pavement was packed with shoppers, either bustling along busily or stopping to look in the brightly lit shop windows. John and Sarah made their way slowly through the crowds until Sarah stepped into a side alley, pulling John in alongside her. 'Let's take a quick rest for a moment, okay?'

John nodded, glancing up and down the quiet street, which was packed only with refuse and bins.

'I still can't believe we got away with that,' she chuckled. 'When they asked you to come, they can't have been expecting anything from you except blind obedience… I guess they really underestimated you. Who knew you had that in you?'

John just gave an embarrassed shrug.

She stepped closer, and John took a step backwards, his back pressing up against the wall. 'I don't think I managed to say thank you,' she whispered, 'for what you did back there.'

'You can thank me later,' he said. 'When this is all over.'

'Still… it was brave of you.' She moved slightly closer.

'It was stupid and reckless,' he muttered, shaking his head slowly.

'Yes, but also brave.' She leaned forwards and kissed him, but this time it was just a peck on the cheek. Then she moved away slightly, looking him in the eyes. 'I wasn't sure how much you really cared for me.'

'I've told you Sarah. You'll always be special to me; I couldn't just leave you to them.' He sighed and looked down, unable to maintain eye contact. 'But that doesn't mean I don't still love my wife.'

Sarah sighed. 'Why do you always have to bring your wife into this?'

John shook his head in disbelief. 'Because I'm married, Sarah. And despite everything, I love her. I may not have been the best husband over the last few days… but I still love her, and that's the truth.'

Sarah gently took his chin, lifting his head up to look at her again. 'And does she still love you, John? Who's going to love *you*?'

John ignored her question and looked longingly into her bright blue eyes. Gently, he ran his fingertips over the cuts on her face, around the bruises on her cheek. 'Does it hurt?' he asked. 'Did they hurt you badly?'

She looked like she was about to say something, and then stopped. 'No machismo bullshit, right?'

'Right.'

'Yes, it hurt. It still does. But it could have been worse. It *would* have been worse if it hadn't been for you, John.'

She moved in closer again, looking to kiss him on the lips, but he stepped to the side. 'Come on,' he said, turning and walking away. 'We should get going.'

She turned and watched in silence as he walked back to the street.

Chapter 20

John let Sarah take him by the hand as they rejoined the people on the street, letting themselves be pulled along with the stream of shoppers as they flowed along between the shops.

'So what now?' he asked. 'We still have the card reader – they still have the card. Somehow, I don't think they're just going to leave it at that.'

'We have to take this fight to them, John.'

'What?' He stopped, turning to face her, forcing the people behind to stop and go around them.

'If we don't, then they get to dictate the terms. Everything happens on their playing fields. They're down… what? Six men?'

John did a quick tally in his mind. That sounded about right.

'We have to strike them, and do it now – do it while they're unstable.'

'But we don't even know where the card is, Sarah'

She squeezed his hand, pulling him along the pavement again. 'Come on, John,' she said with a smile on her face.

'Sarah?' he asked. 'Is there something I don't know?'

'I didn't drive all the way over here by accident,' she replied with a grin.

'What do you mean?' asked John as they carried on down the street. 'Is the smart-card around here somewhere?'

'I think so. I *hope* so.'

'Where exactly?'

'When Watts and the others were holding me, I could hear them talking. I don't think they knew that I can speak Russian.'

'And what where they saying?'

'They were talking about someone they called *The Devil*.'

'The Devil?'

Sarah nodded. Then she gave a little chuckle, inwardly amused at something. 'Between the devil and the deep blue sea,' she muttered to herself.

'I don't understand,' said John.

'I wouldn't expect you to,' replied Sarah. 'But to me, *The Devil* has a certain implication. It could just be coincidence, but there's a Russian businessman who's located not too far from here. He's widely believed to be a high-up member of the *Bratva*, the Russian Mafia, but no one's ever been able to prove it. His moniker in the Russian underground? The Devil.'

'Then you think he's who they're working for? He's the one who's after the smart-card?'

Sarah nodded. 'The one who *has* the smart-card – unless we can get it back.' She stopped, pulling him to a halt in a shop doorway. 'It's not going to be easy, John.' She nodded over towards a large lot on the other side of the road. It was a second-hand car dealership with dozens and dozens of cars all laid out across a considerable area, floodlights keeping them all clearly visible in the dimming afternoon light. A compact garage and workshop stood to one side with a three-storey office building at the rear.

'It'll be in *there* somewhere, and it sure won't be easy to get to it. That's where we'll find The Devil, John. Welcome to Hell.'

Chapter 21

'So do you have a plan?' asked John as they stood in the shop doorway, looking over the road towards the garage opposite.

Sarah just shook her head. 'Not yet. We can't just go in guns blazing – we'd be lucky to make it in alive, never mind back out again.'

'So… what do we do?'

'I want to watch. See their comings and goings; see if I can spot any weaknesses. Try and find some chink in their armour that we can exploit. Most of all… we need to work out exactly where they're keeping the card.'

'And how do you expect to do that?'

'I have an idea… but nothing more than that just yet.' She looked at her watch. It was coming up to four o'clock. 'We need to do some shopping before everywhere shuts.' She looked into her handbag. 'We're getting low on cash… British money, anyway. Come on,' she said, leading him along the road.

She ducked into a travel agent, heading for their Bureaux de Change and stepping up to the counter.

'How can I help you today?' asked the lady behind the window.

'I'd like to change some dollars for some of your English money,' asked Sarah in a perfect west-coast American accent.

'Certainly. How much?'

Sarah thought for a moment. 'Five hundred dollars.' It seemed a reasonable amount; she didn't want to raise too much suspicion by being greedy.

'That will be fine. Do you have any identification?'

She turned to John. 'Do you have any ID, honey? The hotel is still looking after my passport.' She withdrew five hundred-dollar notes from her handbag, slipping them through the small slot under the window.

John pulled out his wallet, removing his driving licence. 'Will this do?'

'That will be fine.' The lady typed looked at the licence, typing the details into her computer. 'That will come to four hundred and two pounds.'

'That's fine,' said Sarah.

The lady opened a drawer and pulled out several notes and two pound coins, counting them out in front of John and Sarah. She pulled a receipt out of a small printer next to the computer, putting the money and the receipt into a paper wallet and slipping it under the window.

Sarah took the money, placing it in her handbag before turning and leaving with John. She led him down the street until they came to a camping and outdoor goods store. Entering and walking past the tents and camping equipment, Sarah headed straight for the jackets. She found two thick black coats with large furry hoods – good for obscuring their faces without drawing attention in the current climate. Then she headed to the back of the store, looking around until she found what she was after: binoculars. She purchased the highest-power set that they sold.

Next she headed to a department store, browsing through the make-up department until she found some foundation that matched her skin tone and a small mirror.

They left and headed to a small café a few doors along. They sat by the window, not talking, just watching the garage and sipping their coffee while the sun slowly set. As they watched, Sarah gently applied the foundation to her face to mask the bruises and cuts on her face. There was only so much she could do, but John still thought she did a reasonable job with what she had.

Once the sun had gone down and dusk had fully descended, they left, putting on their new coats.

'Come with me,' said Sarah. 'We need to find a good vantage point where we can see as much of that place as we can.' She led him down a side alley and then around to the rear of the row of shops. They stood in a small private car park, several cars squeezed into tight spots between large overflowing rubbish bins. She looked about until she saw what she wanted – a set of black metal steps leading up to a rear first-floor doorway.

John followed her up the steps. As she reached the top, she looked around; all around was quiet and they could see no one watching. 'Hold this,' she asked John, passing him her handbag as she climbed up the metal handrail next to the stairs, holding onto the wall. She carefully stood up on the handrail, then reached up, grabbing hold of the metal railings of a fence on the flat root above. She hauled herself up and over, and then leant back down, reaching between the railings. 'Pass me the bags,' she asked, and John obliged, first passing her the handbag and then the bag containing the binoculars.

'You expect me to get up there too?' asked John.

'It's easy,' said Sarah. 'Hold my hand.'

John climbed onto the lowest railing of the handrail, slowly reaching up and then leaning across for Sarah's hand. She held him tight, pulling him up towards her as he stretched upwards, grabbing hold of the railings. Then he let go of her hand, climbing up and over the railings. Sarah switched to reach over the top instead, grabbing hold of his coat and pulling him over.

They stood together on top of the row of shops. The wind was stronger here, making the air seem colder.

'Tread lightly,' said Sarah. 'I don't know who's underneath us. They won't be expecting anyone to be up here.'

She tiptoed slowly and carefully around the edge of the rooftop until she reached the front of the roof from where they could see the garage and forecourt. More floodlights and signs had been turned on around the lot, lighting up the cars so that customers could still view them in the early winter evening. She lay down in the shadows of the roof, pulling out the binoculars.

John came and lay down next to her. 'What are you looking for?'

'At the moment I'm just looking. I want to make sure Alexandrov is in.'

'Alexandrov?'

'*The Devil.* Alexandrov Victorovich.'

She lay there for a while, slowly scanning across the garage forecourt and from window to window across the buildings at the rear. 'Okay,' she eventually said. 'Can you get my phone from my bag?'

John reached inside, pulling out her phone.

'You'll need to turn it on. I don't like walking around with my own personal tracking device active all the time.'

John held down the power button, and waited patiently for it to power itself up.

'It's *five-six-four-six* to unlock it,' she said without taking her eyes from the binoculars, and John typed in the digits. 'There's a phone number for the garage on the sign out front. Can you call it for me, and then put it on speaker-phone?'

John looked over the street at the large sign standing just by the entrance. The name on it was *Rush & Sons Autos*. 'Nice name,' chuckled John. 'Subtle.'

'It's not illegal to be Russian,' said Sarah. 'Just dial the number.'

John typed in the digits and then put it on speaker-phone, placing the phone down close to Sarah's head. It rang a few times before someone answered.

'Rush and Sons Autos,' came a voice with just a hint of a Russian accent. 'How can I help you?'

'I want to talk to Alexandrov Victorovich,' asked Sarah slowly.

'I'm sorry, who?'

'Don't play games. We both know who I'm talking about,' stated Sarah. 'Tell him it's Sarah Hutchinson. Tell him it's about the card reader. Tell him I'm ready to make a deal.'

The voice on the other end muttered something incomprehensible in Russian, and then the line went quiet; they had been put on hold. Sarah continued to observe through the binoculars, looking for movement within the buildings.

A few moments later a new voice came out of the speaker.

'Talk to me.' This was a serious voice with a heavy Russian accent, the voice of someone used to getting what they wanted.

'You have the card, I have the reader,' said Sarah. 'I want to propose a trade.'

A pause. 'What do you want?'

'Fifty thousand. In cash.'

Silence.

'We both know that the information on the card is worth a whole load more than that,' she added. 'I'm willing to take fifty thousand for a quick and painless end to all of this. I just want out. You'll have the card and reader, and we never have to see each other ever again.'

Another pause. 'That is acceptable. You have the card reader on you now?'

'Yes,' replied Sarah. 'At least I have one of them. The one your men tried to liberate from Gabriel Private Bank. I have two different readers hidden away in separate secure locations. If the card matches the reader I have on me now, then we can meet tonight – I'm only an hour away from you. If not… then it will have to be in the morning.'

'So how do we know if you have the correct reader?'

'On front of the card is a set of numbers. Tell me the last four digits. If it matches what I have on my reader, then we're good to go.'

For a moment they heard nothing over the phone. Sarah was holding her breath; it all depended on this.

'Okay,' he said. 'One moment.'

Through the binoculars, Sarah watched Victorovich stand up from behind his desk and walk across his office. She watched him as he lifted a painting off the wall, revealing a safe with a keypad that had been hidden behind it. She watched him type in a combination, opening the safe and reaching inside to pull something out. He was holding a small black card in his hand.

'Four, seven, two, zero,' he read out slowly.

'Let me check…' Sarah paused for a moment, as if she were inspecting her reader. 'Yes. That's a match. We're good to go.'

'Where?'

'Toddington Services on the M1 northbound. We'll be in the far corner of the car park.'

'One hour,' he said.

'One hour,' she confirmed. She removed the binoculars momentarily as she hung up the phone.

Looking through the binoculars again, she watched Victorovich place the card back in the safe, closing the door and rehanging the painting in front of it.

'We've got two hours,' she said to John. 'Well, one hour until they work out we're not there, then another hour for them to get back again.'

'You think they believed you?'

'We'll find out in a moment.' She was still looking intently through the binoculars.

'They'd have that much money to hand?' he asked. 'They'd bring it with them?'

'They'd have that much money,' she explained. 'I had to go for a figure large enough to be plausible, but not so large that they wouldn't have it lying around. As to actually bringing it with them… well, maybe, but I doubt it; I didn't see Victorovich take any money from his safe. But even if they did bring it with them, they'd never let us leave with it. If we went to those services, there's no way we'd ever come out again alive. These men can't be trusted an inch, John. You don't get to be a head honcho in the *Bratva* by giving away money and leaving behind witnesses. You either work for them or you're their enemy, and they never let their enemies go. I believe Brand and Watts were hired mercenaries, nasty but professional nevertheless.'

'Like you used to be?' asked John.

Sarah ignored the question. 'These Russians, on the other hand… these are vicious psychopaths, who'd have no qualms about torturing and killing us. Just remember that.'

She looked out over at the garage. People were on the move, lights going on and off in the offices. She saw the lights go on in two black BMWs that were parked in front of the office, and then they pulled rapidly off the forecourt, heading out into the night.

'That's four more of them gone,' she said, 'including Victorovich.' She picked up her phone and proceeded to turn it off before she dropped it back into her handbag. 'Okay. Time to go. Time to finish this.'

Chapter 22

John and Sarah climbed down off the roof and crept down the steps. It was still quiet and deserted behind the shops.

'Have you still got your gun?' asked Sarah.

John tapped his jacket pocket. 'Still there.'

'Just don't draw it unless you plan to shoot someone, John. Not unless you're willing to kill them. If the Russians see you even holding a gun, they'll shoot to kill. Understand?'

John nodded silently. Sarah reached into his pocket, pulling out the gun. She quickly showed him how the safety worked; she didn't want him unable to shoot at a vital moment.

'One other thing – when we're over there, I need you to do whatever I ask you to do without question. We may need to move fast. I need to know you've got my back.'

John nodded again.

'Then let's go. Stick close.'

They hurried back to the front of the shops, jogging across the road between passing cars. Sarah stopped at the gates to the garage forecourt. There were still lights on in the buildings at the back of the lot and she thought she could sense movement.

She put up her hood, zipping up her jacket and then stepping between the gates, walking from car to car, looking at the price tags on the windscreens and peering through the side windows. She kept one hand on her handbag, John's hand in the other. Slowly and casually, they made their way towards the cars and buildings at the rear of the lot.

As they approached the buildings, a man came out of the open doorway. 'Can I help you?' he asked. His English accent was good, with only a hint of Russian. John hoped it wasn't the same man that Sarah had spoken to on the phone – he didn't want him to recognize her voice.

Sarah pointed towards a red Honda Civic that was sitting next to her. 'This says four grand,' she said, indicating the price stuck on the windscreen. 'Will you do thirty-seven fifty?' She turned to John. 'That's our limit, right, honey?'

'Yes,' agreed John 'That's as high as we can go.'

The man thought for a second, then smiled, a wide beaming smile. 'Sure, for you, I'm sure we can do that. Have you got any questions you want to ask about it?'

'Warranty?'

'Six months.'

Sarah nodded. 'Sounds good. Do you offer credit?'

The man nodded back. 'We offer very competitive terms. Do you want to come into the office to discuss it?'

Sarah took John by the hand. 'That sounds great. Come on, honey.'

Together they followed the man into the lair of The Devil.

The salesman led them through the door and into a small office, indicating towards a couple of chairs in front of the desk where they could sit. He turned, walking to the side of the office and opening a filing cabinet, which he quickly flicked through until he found what he wanted, pulling out a set of forms.

John and Sarah sat down in the chairs, lowering their hoods.

The salesman turned back, sitting behind the desk and laying down the paperwork in front of them. He picked up a pen, clicking the end to extract the tip. 'I trust you have some form of identification?'

'Sure,' replied Sarah. She reached into her handbag, pulling out one of the passports, placing it on the desk next to her, but not offering it to him. John shuffled uncomfortably in his chair.

Sarah looked at the papers that the man had laid out in front of her, running her finger down the side of the page as she pretended to read through the text. 'What does this mean here?' she asked, pointing to some small-print at the bottom of the page, a quizzical look on her face.

The salesman stood up, leaning over the desk towards them. 'Let me have a look,' he muttered, reaching for the papers.

As he looked down, Sarah leapt up, grabbing him by the hair on top of his head, slamming his head down hard into the desk. His head bounced up again, his nose broken and bleeding. As he started to panic and pull back, Sarah reached for a paperweight on the desk, an ornate glass globe about the size of a baseball with a pattern of crystal shapes inside. She swung it ferociously at his head, hitting him hard on the temple.

The man fell back, tumbling sideways out of his chair and falling to the floor. Sarah darted around to his side of the desk, kneeling down next to him. He was out cold, his face a bloody mess. Sarah felt for the pulse on his carotid artery. It was still beating; he was merely unconscious, not dead.

John had only just risen out of his chair. It had all happened so fast.

Sarah held one finger to her lips, motioning him to be quiet. They both stood still in the small office, listening intently. They could hear no one coming, no alarms sounding, no angry shouts.

There was a telephone on the desk, and Sarah grabbed it, ripping the cable from the wall. She used the plastic wire to tie his hands behind his back and then shoved his body into the small space under the desk. Then she stepped around the desk, moving to the door where she turned around the sign hanging in the window so that from the outside it now read *Closed*.

There was a single door out of the office, labelled with an *Employees Only* sign. Sarah stepped over to it, taking both her pistol and the silencer from her bag, patiently screwing the silencer into the end of the barrel. She took a deep breath and then took hold of the handle, twisting it. The door was unlocked, and it opened into a short corridor.

There were two white wooden doors on either side, and at the far end was a set of stairs leading up. The closest door on the left was standing open. They could hear a radio playing within; from where they stood, it looked like a small kitchen.

Sarah gestured to John that they were heading upstairs, and started cautiously down the corridor. They reached the steps unchallenged, and Sarah headed upwards. She kept close to the wall, John following in her footsteps.

At the top of the steps, the passageway turned around one hundred and eighty degrees, heading back the way they had come. This floor seemed to have the same layout as the floor below –two doors either side, although these all stood open. At the end was another set of stairs leading up. That was where Victorovich's office was located.

Sarah had only taken a couple of steps along the corridor when a man stepped out of the doorway to her right. He was tall and wiry, dressed in jeans and a tight white t-shirt, his hair black and shoulder length. He was stood just a few feet away and obviously surprised to see them.

She raised her gun towards him, but he reacted with lightning reflexes, reaching out and knocking the gun from her hands. With her gun skidding away on the floor, she aimed a punch at him, but he stepped effortlessly to the side, grabbing her hand within one of his own and twisting her arm. She leant over, lessening the force, and as she did so she swept one leg across the hallway. It connected with his just below the knee, chopping his support away from underneath him. He didn't fall, but he did stagger backwards, releasing his grip on her hand.

She tried to use this to her advantage, moving forwards with a series of roundhouse kicks – first with her right leg then with her left – but both times he jumped nimbly backwards, out of her range.

She tried again, but this time she was pushing her luck. The man stepped to the side, knocking her leg away. She stumbled, and this time he advanced, stepping forwards to punch her in the gut. She doubled over and he advanced, moving in close and sending another one-two of blows into either side of her torso.

He punched again, but she managed to block this blow with her arm, knocking his fist to the side. She straightened up, and as she did so she raised one leg, her knee rising violently into his groin.

He bent forwards, an expression of pain on his face and Sarah grabbed hold of his head by the hair, one hand on either side of his face. With all her might, she brought up her knee again, smashing it into this face even as she held it firm in her hands.

The blow ripped his head away, leaving clumps of hair in her hands. He staggered backwards and Sarah stepped forwards, swinging her arm in a powerful arc. It connected with his chin and he flew backwards, landing with a thump on the floor. She stepped forwards, leaning over him, ready to power a kick into his head, but he wasn't moving; he was already unconscious.

She looked up to see another man standing in the doorway ten feet from her. This man had short black hair and was dressed in a black suit on top of a white shirt. He was holding a gun in his hand. It was pointed directly at her.

There was a loud crack of a gunshot. Sarah winced, expecting the worst, but there was no pain. Instead, the man in the suit staggered backwards, dropping to his knees and then falling forwards to the floor. There was a large red stain on the front of his shirt, and an even larger hole in his back.

She turned around to see John standing behind her, a smoking gun in his hand. His face was white and pale; he looked like he was in shock.

Sarah stepped quickly to him, gently taking hold of his hands and carefully taking the gun from him. 'Shush,' she whispered soothingly. 'It's okay.' Then she stepped back, giving him a sharp slap to the cheek. He flinched, shaking his head.

'You can process this later,' she added. 'But for now we've got to keep moving.' She reached down, picking up her gun from the floor. 'So much for the silencer,' she muttered. 'We need to be quick.'

She grabbed John by the hand, pulling him forwards. He followed without thinking, following her up the next staircase.

As they arrived on the second floor two doors opened, one on either side of the corridor. A man emerged from the door on the left with a gun in his hand and Sarah let loose two bullets without thinking, the crack of the shots muffled by the silencer. Both shots hit the man in the chest and before he had even hit the floor, she twisted and fired two more rounds, dropping the second man as he was still drawing his gun from his shoulder holster. She waited a few seconds, listening for sounds of anyone else before she grabbed John with her left hand and headed straight for the door that was their destination. She grabbed the handle and turned it, relieved to find it unlocked.

They were in Victorovich's office. Time was of the essence now, and she ignored everything apart from the painting on the wall, running straight for it. She ripped the picture from the wall, throwing it across the room. In front of her stood the safe.

'Do you know the combination?' asked John.

Sarah turned. He seemed to be coming out of his daze, slowly rubbing his cheek.

'Do you know it?' he repeated.

'I think so,' she replied. 'The first two numbers for definite, the third number probably. I'm not sure about the last. I think it was in the top right, but he was moving about and he obscured my vision temporarily. It may take a few attempts.'

She typed in the first two numbers, *one-zero*, then *nine*. She thought for a second, and then pressed *five*.

There was a buzz and a red cross lit up under the keypad. There were two more dark crosses next to it.

'*Shit*,' she cursed.

'What?'

'It looks like I only get three goes.'

She tried again. *One-zero-nine-six*. Another buzz, and the second of three crosses appeared.

'What happens if we get it wrong again?' asked John.

'I don't know. Maybe it locks us out for an hour. Maybe it sets off an alarm. Fuck.' Sarah swallowed and closed her eyes. She took a deep breath and then opened her eyes again. She keyed in *One-zero-nine-*

'Three,' said John.

'What?'

'Three,' he repeated.

'Why three?'

'Just a guess,' he said. 'It's as good as any other number.'

'So why suggest it?'

'It's when we first met. October nineteen ninety-three.'

Sarah shrugged and pressed *three*. This time there was a click and the door popped open. She grabbed at the handle, yanking it open. Inside there were several bundles of cash and some sheets of paper. Resting on top of the cash sat the black smart-card. She picked up the cash and the card, dropping them into her handbag.

'Let's get the hell out of here,' she said. She took John by the hand again, her gun in the other, running out of the room and down the stairs.

As she neared the door back to the front office, another man stepped out of a doorway. Sarah swung the gun in her hand, pistol-whipping the man on the side of the head. He dropped like a stone.

They ignored him as he lay moaning on the floor, and ran through the office and out into the night.

Chapter 23

'I can't believe we've done it,' exclaimed John as he drove the van along the busy London roads. It was late now, the Friday-night partiers and revellers starting to pack the streets.

'All thanks to you,' smiled Sarah. 'I couldn't have done it without you.' She leaned over, giving him a little peck on the cheek before sitting back and gazing out of her side window. They were driving along the embankment, the river Thames visible behind the railings at the side of the pavement. 'Pull over,' she said suddenly.

John slowed the van, pulling up onto the pavement and stopping. 'What is it?'

Sarah leaned over next to him, running her hand across his chest and then into his jacket pocket, pulling out the pistol. She sat back, wiping it with a cloth before picking up a plastic bag from the floor and dropping the gun into it.

'What are you doing?' asked John.

'Getting rid of the evidence.' She opened the door and marched across to the edge of the pavement overlooking the river. She lifted the bag behind her shoulder, throwing it with all her might and it flew through the air, landing well into the river and disappearing without trace. Then she turned and trotted back to the van.

'What now?' asked John.

'We need to stay somewhere for the night. First thing in the morning we'll go to MI6. I'll hand myself in with the card and the reader – that and my knowledge of my handlers should be enough to convince them that I am who I say I am.'

'And you'll be okay?'

'I'll be just fine.' She flashed him a wide smile. 'I'll make sure your part in all of this is appreciated too.'

'I don't need any recognition,' he replied.

'Hey, if you don't want to be the hero, that's fine,' she said. 'But you may like someone from MI6 to speak to the police on your behalf, make sure there aren't any *misunderstandings*.'

In the heat of the moment, John hadn't really considered this. He'd been too caught up in everything, but she was right, of course. 'Yeah, I think that might be useful,' he replied. He thought for a moment. 'So where are we planning to spend the night then? Presumably not in the back of this van again?'

Sarah reached into her handbag, pulling out the money she had taken from Victorovich's safe. It looked like at a lot of money – tens of thousands of pounds. 'I say we find the biggest, fanciest hotel we can.'

They checked into the Savoy Hotel as Mr and Mrs Butler, using Sarah's fake passport as identification, and took the largest suite they had available. This was much more than just a normal hotel room, with its own spacious bathroom, living room and small kitchenette in addition to the large master bedroom.

They didn't have any luggage, and so took themselves up to the room and let themselves in. John was amazed at the size and quality of the room, but he supposed that at fifteen hundred pounds a night, it ought to be pretty bloody luxurious. He slipped off his jacket and shoes, putting them away by the door before going to the bathroom and washing his hands and face. It felt good to wash away the dirt and grime of the previous few days.

When he was feeling slightly more himself, he came out of the bathroom. He couldn't see Sarah in the living room, so instead stepped into the bedroom.

She was lying on the bed, dressed in only her underwear. 'I've been waiting for you,' she purred seductively.

'Sarah, I can't do this,' muttered John, although he desperately wished he could.

She rolled over, climbing across the bed and standing up to face him. She stepped closer and looked John straight in the eyes. 'This will probably be our last night together,' she whispered. She wrapped her arms around his waist, pulling him in closer. Her face was right next to his and she gently kissed his ear. 'Whatever you want...'

'My wife...' whispered John.

Sarah pulled away slightly to look him in the face. 'I'd be up for it,' she teased, 'but I'm not sure she'd be interested in joining us.'

Their lips were almost touching, and John could feel her warm breath on his face. Despite everything, he still longed for her touch.

'I owe you,' she murmured. 'I'll do whatever you want, something to remember me by.'

She sunk downwards, her hands slipping down his back until they were on his buttocks and she was on her knees. Then she brought her hands around and started to undo his belt.

'No,' said John, taking a half-step backwards and pushing her gently away.

'Really?' she purred, looking up at him. 'I can tell you still want me. You've never been able to say no to me.' She licked her lips demurely.

'Not this time,' he said, stepping away further. 'I love my wife.'

'But she doesn't love you any more, John. She doesn't want you... I do.'

'But... I've got to try... and this isn't going to help.'

Sarah looked up at John and sighed. She could see from the look in his eyes that this time he meant it. Slowly, she stood up.

'Well, I can't say I'm not disappointed,' she sighed. 'But maybe you've earned a little respect. You've finally grown yourself a backbone.'

She turned, so that she was no longer facing him. 'You can sleep on the couch out there,' she said. 'I'm taking the bed.'

John spent the night alone and undisturbed on the sofa. It was really quite comfy, better than a lot of hotel beds he had slept in over the years. He rose early in the morning, getting himself dressed and making himself a cup of coffee while he waited for Sarah to rouse herself.

She eventually emerged from the bedroom fully naked, stepping across into the bathroom. John wondered if she was trying to entice him, or if she just didn't care. 'I'm taking a shower,' she called. Was that meant to be an invitation? If so, he wasn't going to bite. The hotel had delivered a morning paper and instead he briefly read through the front page before heading for the crossword.

Five minutes later, Sarah emerged from the bathroom, still completely naked but now glistening and wet, beads of moisture running down her skin. Her hands were held up above her head, ostensibly to dry her hair with a towel, but probably more to raise and accentuate the curve of her breasts.

'So, do you have any ideas for what you want to do?' she asked. She was definitely doing this on purpose. Either she still fancied one final fling, or else she was just teasing him, playing with him for spurning her the previous night.

With incredible inner strength, John took his eyes off her and returned to the crossword. 'I thought we were going to MI6, handing in the smartcard.'

He needed every last part of his willpower not to look at her as he heard her walk away to the bedroom, closing the door behind her. He sighed, and hoped he hadn't pissed her off. She wouldn't be a good woman to be on the wrong side of.

But when the bedroom door re-opened a couple of minutes later and she emerged fully dressed and made-up, she seemed fine. 'Let me grab a coffee myself, and then we can go,' she suggested. She looked at John reading the papers. 'Anything about us in there?'

'Not that I've seen.' He stood up, moving over to the kitchen area to make himself some toast.

'They're probably trying to keep it quiet for now. Not sure how long they can keep it hushed up for, though. Too many witnesses, too many dead bodies.'

She joined him in the kitchen, pouring herself a cup of the coffee, smiling as she sipped it; it was good. 'Are you good to go?' she asked a few moments later, when she had drained the mug.

'Almost,' replied John. 'I haven't finished my toast yet.'

Sarah leaned forwards across the table, picking up the half slice of toast from his plate and greedily taking a bite out of it.

'Hey!' cried John in mock anger.

Sarah quickly wolfed down the last few bites, before licking her fingers clean.

'Come on,' she said with a cheeky grin. 'Let's go be heroes.'

They checked themselves out of the hotel, paying for the room with Victorovich's cash before returning to their van. Sarah insisted that John drive, and they set off for the MI6 headquarters in Vauxhall Cross, located just off the embankment.

As they approached the end of the street, she asked him to stop the van, and he pulled over to the side of the road. 'I'll do the last bit myself,' she said. 'I could do with some fresh air and a moment to prepare myself. It might be quite an intense debriefing.'

'They're not going to hurt you, are they?' asked John. 'Torture you?'

'Of course not,' replied Sarah. 'But they will thoroughly interrogate me to ensure I am who I say I am. Make sure I'm on the level.'

'Oh. Okay,' said John.

'Do me a favour,' asked Sarah. She pulled a pen and notepad from the glove compartment of the car. On it, she quickly jotted down an address. 'Take the van back to here and leave it on the drive, will you? The owner will be back from their holiday in a couple of days.'

'What, you don't want me to torch it?' he asked with a little chuckle. 'Dump it in the river?'

'I was thinking of you. Thought you'd probably want to do the right thing; the *polite* thing.'

John smiled. 'I suppose so.'

Sarah opened the door, climbing out into the street, but she didn't shut the door just yet.

'We had fun, didn't we?'

'Yes.'

'Just like old times.'

'Not *exactly* like old times,' replied John with a smile.

'We're probably never going to see each other again,' said Sarah.

There was an awkward silence as neither of them said anything. He knew she was leaving him a space, giving him a chance to say whatever he needed to say.

He desperately wanted to tell her to stay. To tell her he loved her. Instead, 'Goodbye, Sarah,' was all he said.

Sarah nodded her head mournfully. 'Goodbye, John.'

She closed the door and set off down the street, her handbag over her shoulder. John watched her go. He knew he was doing the right thing, but still wondered if he would come to regret it.

No, this was for the best, he told himself. He belonged with Amy. He needed to see her again.

Just as soon as he had returned the van.

Chapter 24

John turned the key in the lock and pushed his front door open.

Amy was standing at the other end of the hall. 'You're alive,' she remarked with obvious relief.

John smiled. She still felt *something* for him then. He took a step towards her. 'It's over,' he said. 'She's gone.'

'Forever?'

'Absolutely.'

He took another step forwards, then another. Then he ran to her, wrapping his arms around her, embracing her. She didn't hug him back, simply placing her hands on his hips, but neither did she hit him and scream at him to get out. It was *something*, something he could build on at least, to try and rebuild their fractured relationship.

He wasn't sure how long he stood there with her in his arms before he let go, stepping back to look her in the eyes.

'I'm so sorry,' he sobbed.

'Are you though, John?'

'Yes,' he stated simply. 'I know I've made some bad decisions… choices I'm going to have to live with. I know I've let you down, and for that I'm truly sorry. But I also know that it's you I want.'

'You don't want to be the husband of a spy? Off on secret missions every week?' Behind the anger, he thought he could detect a trace of humour in her voice.

'No. I want you, Amy. I don't know what I can ever do to make it up to you… but I want to try.' He dropped to his knees, looking up at her. 'What do you say, Amy? Do you think we can still try and make this work?'

She started to shake her head and John's heart sank, but then she spoke. 'I must be mad for even considering this… but I think that maybe this is worth one more try.'

John reached out a hand, and she took it, pulling him up.

'Just promise me one thing, John.'

'What is it?'

'That she's out of your life for good now, that you'll never see her again.'

'Absolutely.' He wrapped his arms around her, hugging her like it was their very first time again. This time, she put her hands on his back too. It wasn't passionate, but it *was* progress.

Their embrace was rudely interrupted by a loud knock at the door. John let go of his wife and turned to see who it was. He had left the front door open, and in the doorway there now stood a serious-looking man with a grey moustache and a matching grey suit. Behind him stood a uniformed police officer; not just a constable, this man looked senior.

'Mr Garner?' asked the man in the suit. 'We need to talk.'

'Won't you come in?' asked Amy.

The two men stepped through the doorway, closing the door behind them, and Amy led them into the living room, John trailing behind.

Amy took a seat on the sofa and John came over to sit down next to his wife, holding her hand. He had suspected that the last few days would catch up with him sooner or later; he just hadn't expected it to be quite so soon. He'd hoped for at least a short while with his family before he was arrested.

The man in the suit pulled up a wooden chair opposite him, while the uniformed policeman stood up straight behind him, holding his hat in his hands. 'Mr Garner,' he started.

'John,' said John. 'Call me John.'

'Very well, John. You can call me Michael.'

John's mood lifted slightly. If they were on first name terms already, maybe his outlook wasn't quite as bleak as he had thought. Maybe they had even come to thank him for all the help he had given Sarah in retrieving the information.

Michael took a wallet from his pocket, opening it and retrieving a card from with. He passed it to John. 'My identification. Check it, make sure it's genuine. It's important you believe I am who I say I am.'

John took the laminated ID card and inspected it. It stated that Michael was in fact Michael King, Chief of Operations at MI6. John turned the card around in his hands, looking at it closely. There was a holographic stamp on the rear, intricate watermarks embedded on the photograph of the man sitting before him now. He ran his fingers over the card; some of the identification codes were embossed.

John passed it back again. 'It certainly looks real, but I'm no expert.'

Michael nodded. 'Chief Superintendent Goddard here can also vouch for me.' The man standing behind him gave a solemn nod. 'For now at least, can we proceed on the assumption that I am who my ID asserts me to be?'

John nodded. 'Why are you here?'

'We've come to speak to you about Sarah Hutchinson.'

John could see Amy close her eyes and sigh, shaking her head slightly at the mention of her name. He nodded solemnly back to Michael. 'I know all about her.'

Michael shook his head slowly. 'I'm sorry, but I don't believe you do.'

John smiled weakly. 'It's okay, she told me everything. I know she's a spy. I know she worked for you.'

Michael shook his head again, slowly and deliberately. 'She *is* a spy, John. But she doesn't work for me.' He took a deep breath. 'She's not on our side, John.'

❈ ❈ ❈

'What?' spluttered John. 'I don't understand. Are you saying she's a *foreign* spy?'

Michael nodded.

'She said she worked for someone called Henry Sandford. She said he was her handler at MI6. She said he'd been killed.'

Michael gave a slow, sad nod. 'That's partly true. Henry did work for me in MI6. He was the one overseeing the retrieval of the smart-card for me.'

'And now he's dead?'

Michael nodded. 'She wasn't lying about that either. He was shot and killed in cold blood while he was meeting with one of our agents. He was meant to be meeting up to receive the smart-card when both he and our agent were shot. John… we think that *she* killed both of them.'

Amy shook her head, tears now flowing down her cheeks. 'She played you for a fucking *fool*, John.'

John ignored her, focusing on Michael. 'But I took her to MI6. This morning – I took her to your headquarters on the embankment.'

'Did you, though?' asked Michael.

'I dropped her off outside.'

'But did you actually see her go inside, John? Did you see her talk to anyone? Did you see her give the smart-card to anyone?'

John shook his head. He had to admit that he hadn't.

'Who exactly *is* she working for then?'

'We're not quite sure who she's working for. She's pretty much a gun-for-hire these days. We think it's the Chinese, but we're not one hundred per cent certain.'

'It's not the Russians,' said John. 'They've been consistently trying to kill her. *Us.* They were after the smart-card.'

Another small nod from Michael. 'There's more than one party at play here. There's a whole host of countries who would find that information invaluable. We have to stop them.'

'Then what do you want from me?'

'We need that smart-card back, John. She's got it, and we can't let her get away with it.'

'But what do you expect me to do about it?'

'You know her – probably better than anyone by the looks of it. We need you to help us catch her.'

'No,' muttered Amy, shaking her head.

'I can't,' sighed John.

'John,' said Michael. 'For the last few days, you have been aiding a foreign power in the act of stealing state secrets. You've been involved in whole catalogue of crimes, including espionage, treason… and murder.'

John's head dropped, his shoulders slumping. 'Exactly what are you saying here?' He was starting to fear the worst.

'John,' said Michael. 'You can either be the hero or the villain of this little drama. Based on the events so far, I could take you away right now. With the current political climate, I could detain you indefinitely as an enemy of the state. You would never see your wife again, or your daughter. You would spend the rest of your life in a cold, cramped cell. Or you could step up and do what is required of you, for your Queen and Country.'

John shook his head slowly in disbelief. Amy was quietly sobbing next to him. 'You're not giving me much of a choice, are you?' he eventually said.

'You always have a choice,' replied Michael. 'What kind of country would this be if we didn't at least give you a choice?'

John closed his eyes and sighed, his dead dropping even lower over his lap. 'What exactly do you need me to do?'

'We need you to help us track her down, to help us find her before she leaves the country. You've been with her; you know how she's thinking better than any of my analysts or informants.' He sighed and shook his head. 'My guys have been on their back feet through all of this, while foreign agents have been shooting their way across London. When this is all over, I'm going to have to let a lot of people go.' He stood up. 'Are you in?'

'Yes,' muttered John, still bent forwards with his head in his hands.

'And you, Mrs Garner?'

'What about me?'

'I realize that you have been much more of an innocent party in all of this than your husband… but we would… *I* would be very grateful for your assistance too.'

'How can *I* be of any help?' she asked.

'You've also spent time with her recently. Not as much time, and maybe not quite as intimate, but there still may be things that you noticed that your husband didn't.' John could feel his face reddening. 'Who knows, maybe a feminine perspective of your events of the last few days may turn out to be of importance. It may even help towards some leniency with your husband.'

'Well,' she muttered. 'I suppose if it could help…'

Michael stood up, rubbing his hands together. 'Very well, we should get going.'

'Olivia,' said John suddenly. 'What about our daughter?'

'She's at my sister's house,' explained Amy. 'I asked her to look after her until… well, until this is all over.'

'If it would put your mind at ease,' suggested Michael, 'we could put an undercover car outside their house? Keep an eye on them? Not that I expect anything to happen at this late stage.'

'We'd really appreciate that,' said Amy. She picked up a pad of paper and a pen, scribbling down the address, ripping the page from the pad.

Michael took the sheet of paper, passing it to Chief Superintendent Goddard who was still standing behind him. 'I'll go and sort this out,' he said, stepping back out into the hallway.

'Okay,' said Michael. 'Let's go.'

Chapter 25

They stepped outside to see a large black Range Rover with tinted windows parked outside their house, the engine running. A serious-looking man in a black suit and dark glasses was standing guard next to the rear doors. Chief Superintendent Goddard was sitting in the passenger seat of a grey BMW behind it, talking into a radio.

'If you'll come with me,' said Michael, walking down their driveway at a brisk pace. John and Amy followed, shutting and locking the door behind them.

The man in the suit opened the rear door and Michael climbed inside. John and Amy followed after him, and then the door was shut behind them. The interior of the car was smart and well organized. Two rows of rear seats were positioned facing each other, so that the passengers could have a conversation more efficiently.

The car pulled away without any instructions from Michael. The driver wasn't hanging around, moving away at speed, hidden blue lights in the front and rear flashing away and allowing him to cut through the traffic with a minimum of effort.

'Where are we going?' asked John.

'Back to London, I'm afraid,' explained Michael. 'It's where we believe the handover will be taking place. SIGINT picked up some chatter that we think relates to an exchange of goods. We don't know for certain… but it's our only lead at the moment. This evening, somewhere in London – but that's still a huge area. We've got everyone we can spare looking for her, but it's still a needle in a haystack. I need to be there to oversee the operation, so I'm afraid you'll need to come with me for now. We don't have much time and I need every bit of information you may have for me. Tell me, last time you saw her, did she still have blond, shoulder-length hair?'

John nodded, and then thought for a moment, recalling something. 'She had another British passport,' he said. 'In fact she had two. One of them was in the name Lucy Butler, but the one I'm thinking of was in the name of Marie Mathews. She said that that one was clean – had never been used, in fact. In it, she had dark hair, cut into a short bob.'

'*Good*,' said Michael. 'If that's the cover she's going to use to flee the country, she may already have changed her hair colour to match. We'll get them to consider dark hair as well.' He paused for a moment. 'I don't suppose you would know the numbers on either of those passports?'

'No,' said John with a shake of his head.

'Well, never mind,' added Michael. 'We'll get a flag raised for anyone travelling under either of those names.' He pulled out a large smart-phone, and started typing rapidly into it, sending off a message. When he had finished, he looked up at John and Amy again. 'Now, either of you,' said Michael. 'Is there anything – *anything* – she said which might give us a hint as to where this exchange might be taking place?'

John thought for a second. 'No,' he said grimly with a shake of his head. Amy also gave her head a short sharp shake.

'Take your time,' said Michael. 'This is important. Think back for me. Anything she might have said.'

John closed his eyes, trying to revisit all his adventures of the last few days. 'I'm sorry,' he eventually sighed. 'I can't think of anything. We were always just trying to get through whatever immediate crisis we were currently in. There was never anything mentioned apart from turning it over to MI6.'

Michael shrugged. 'Okay. Just tell me what you can, then. Tell me everything that she's done since you met her again.'

John told him. He told him as much as he could recall, although with Amy sitting next to him he skipped over some of the more intimate moments. It took almost an hour, and when he had finished, he sat back in his seat and sighed.

'And that's the last you saw of her? In the street next to our offices?'

John nodded.

'That could just be her trying to keep her cover story up… or it could mean that that's roughly where she needs to be. The exchange could be somewhere on the embankment.' He frantically typed into his phone again, sending another message.

'So…' said John when Michael had finished typing his latest update. 'I know you probably can't tell me… but I need to ask anyway. What's on that smart-card?'

Michael leaned back in his seat. He said nothing for a short while; he seemed to be thinking intently. Eventually he just sighed. 'I'm sure I shouldn't tell you, but it seems to be about the only part of this whole sordid affair you don't already know.

'The card contains the secret keys for most of the encrypted messages we send to our agents in the field. If an enemy power gets their hands on those keys, then they would be able to read any message they intercept. Not just current messages, but historic ones too – all kinds of secrets that could be embarrassing or dangerous to this country. Not only that, but they would be able to send messages to our agents too, indistinguishable from genuine instructions. We're changing what we can as quickly as we can, but there's a limit to what we can do, especially with the agents currently in the field. We absolutely cannot let those keys fall into the wrong hands if we can possibly help it.' He breathed out a long sorrowful sigh. 'I can't help but feel, however, that we've already failed.'

John sat in silence for five minutes, staring out the window. The car had pulled off the motorway to take a short-cut around some substantial queues up ahead; the road had been closed because of a serious accident. He didn't recognize the road they were on and he wondered exactly where they were. Then it struck him; Sarah's microtransmitter.

'I've got a way you may be able find her,' he suddenly blurted out.

Michael turned round to look at him. 'Tell me.'

'I told you about the microtransmitter that Sarah used to track me down, and to track down my wallet?'

Michael nodded. He could sense were this was going.

'I last time I saw that, it was in Sarah's handbag. She probably still has it on her. If it's still just sitting at the bottom of the handbag, I suppose it's unlikely you'll be able track it… but it's got to be worth a try, surely?'

'But without the matching receiver, it's useless,' said Michael.

'I'm not sure,' said John, 'but I think it's still in the van. When I dumped it, I emptied the back of the van, but I forgot to empty the glove box. I *think* it's still there.'

'And where's the van?'

John reached into his pocket, pulling out the slip of paper that Sarah had given him; the address of where to return the van. 'I left it here,' he said. 'This is where she stole it from in the first place.'

Michael nodded. He took the slip of paper and started typing rapidly into his phone again. 'I'll get someone over there right now. It's definitely worth a try.'

They descended into silence again as they waited nervously for an update. It took ten minutes for the first message to come through to his phone, confirming that they had found the receiver in the van's glove box as hoped. So far they had been unable to pick up any signal from the transmitter, however.

They carried on south towards London, back on the M1 again and heading past Luton.

John jumped as Michael's phone buzzed into life. 'Talk to me,' he said casually as he accepted the call. He nodded to himself as he listened patiently. 'Okay,' he said eventually, 'everyone to centre on that location. Spread out, standard search pattern.' He hung up, placing the phone back in his lap.

'We've just got a single ping from the transmitter,' he explained. 'South of the river, just outside Putney.' He knocked on the glass window separating the front of the car from the rear and it slowly rolled down. 'When we get to London, head for Putney,' he said, and the driver nodded by way of reply.

The Range Rover slowly crawled across Putney Bridge before Michael tapped on the glass and indicated to the driver that he should pull over. The driver obliged, pulling the vehicle to the side of the road, its discreet blue lights still flashing.

'I'm afraid we'll need to let you out here,' said Michael. 'We can't just pull civilians into the centre of an active investigation. It doesn't work that way in the real world.'

'Not a problem,' said Amy, and John agreed.

'Whichever way this goes tonight, we're going to need to talk to you again,' said Michael. 'We've booked you both a room for the night in the Belgrove Hotel – it's not the finest hotel in London, but we're working with a limited budget. Someone will collect you first thing in the morning for an official debriefing.' He stepped out onto the pavement, John and Amy following close behind. As he stepped out into the street, he held out his arm to flag down a passing black cab. It pulled over next to them, and the driver rolled the window down.

'Where to, mate?' asked the cabby.

'I need you to take these two to the Belgrove Hotel,' said Michael. 'There should be a room booked in your names,' he added to John and Amy. Then he took out his wallet and pulled out several ten pound notes, which he passed through the window. 'This ought to cover it.' The taxi driver nodded appreciatively, and Amy opened the back door, climbing in. John climbed in after her and then Michael leant into the cab after them.

John turned to look at him, and saw that he was holding out a business card. On it was simply the name *Michael King* and a mobile number. 'If you remember anything, give me a call.'

'Will do,' said John.

'I hope you catch the bitch,' added Amy.

Chapter 26

John and Amy were sitting in the back of the taxi on their way to the hotel. They had been travelling for a few minutes and neither had said a word to the other yet. They were both ignoring the awkward silence and instead just looking out of their windows.

Suddenly, John jerked upright in his seat. 'The deep blue sea...' he muttered to himself.

'What?' asked Amy.

'Stop the car!' he barked at the taxi driver.

'But I was paid to take you to the hotel.'

'Just stop the fucking car,' shouted John. The taxi driver obliged, pulling over sharply to the side of the road.

'Take *her* to the hotel,' he told the driver, this time in a more level-headed voice. He pulled out his wallet, pulling out some notes and passing them to the driver. 'Just make sure she gets there – I'm getting out here.'

'What is it, John?' asked Amy, the fear clear in her voice. 'What's the matter?'

'There's something I need to check,' he said. 'But I need you to get going. If this is what I think it might be, I don't want you anywhere near here.'

'Screw that,' she hissed. 'I'm coming with you, John.'

He shook his head slowly. 'It's too dangerous, Amy.'

He started to open the door and climb out, but she grabbed him by the arm. 'You need to start trusting me, John. You need to start being honest with me. We're meant to be married – for better or for worse, right? Anything you have to do, we can do it together.'

'You mean that?'

She swallowed. 'I think so. Just don't make me regret this.'

He nodded. 'Keep the money, mate,' he said to the taxi driver. 'Sorry for the inconvenience.'

They both climbed out, shutting the door behind them and the taxi pulled out, accelerating back into the flow of traffic.

'So what is it?' asked Amy. 'Why are we standing here in the middle of nowhere?'

They were standing by the side of the road near the embankment, old factories and offices on either side of the road. In front of them stood an old abandoned office block; written in large white letters on the side of the building was *Deep Blue Sea Marine Services*.

John and Amy carefully crept towards the old building, which stood in ruins before them.

'When I was with Sarah,' explained John, 'she knew where the Russians were holed up, where they were keeping the smart-card. She called the man who had it *The Devil*. She thought it was funny at the time, and murmured something about *The Devil and the Deep Blue Sea*. I'd forgotten all about it, until I saw that sign.' He gestured up to the huge name on the side of the building.

'So what do you think?'

'I don't know. It can't just be a coincidence though, right? It's got to mean something, *surely*. Maybe it's a safe house for her. Maybe it's where she's meeting whoever she's working for. This could be where she's going to make the exchange.'

'And you're going to stop her? This is a job for the police, John – a job for the security services.'

John shook his head in frustration. 'This is only a hunch. Maybe it *is* just a coincidence. But I need to check. If it turns out she is here, then we can call Michael or the police. I don't want to call them away from the actual search on a wild good chase.'

'Okay…' said Amy uncertainly. 'But let's just take it carefully, okay? This isn't your fight any more.'

John nodded. 'Slowly and carefully. Got it.'

The main building was set back from the road, and they had to creep along the edge of a wide car park to get close to it. The doorways may have once been sealed up, but at least one now stood open, a large dark opening with no remains of any door. John approached carefully, Amy following closely behind.

When he reached the doorway, he peered carefully inside, and when he saw no one, he stepped through. The ground floor of the building looked gutted. There was a large open expanse before them, occasionally punctuated with thick concrete pillars. Around the edges stood the occasional room: some empty offices, and stairwells leading up. There was no one visible in here, and nowhere to hide.

John stood still, listening intently. Maybe it was his imagination, but he thought he could hear noises from above; it sounded like echoing footsteps. Fifty feet to his left was a stairwell, and he headed for it. All that remained within were bare concrete steps, any carpets or handrails long gone, but that was all he needed. Slowly, he started to ascend.

Halfway up, he turned to see Amy still standing at the bottom of the stairs, looking up at him.

'Are you coming?' he whispered.

She shook her head.

'Come on,' he whispered again. 'I need to see if anyone is up here.'

Amy sighed and started to follow him up the stairs. As he reached the landing, he slowed, peering out through the open doorway. This level wasn't gutted like the floor below, but neither was it in a good state of repair. Through the doorway he could see interior walls, partitions that formed a corridor. Open doorways opened into what must have once been offices but were now just dark empty shells. He was also more certain now that there was someone up here; he could hear voices in the distance.

'John!' hissed Amy.

'What?'

'We should go. It's not safe.'

'I need to be sure it's her. It could be just anyone – homeless people wanting some shelter or kids looking for somewhere to hang out and drink or do drugs.' He crept forwards, keeping low and moving towards the cover of a couple of old wooden desks that stood abandoned in the corridor.

'John!' hissed Amy again, in what was meant to be a whisper. She pulled her phone out of her pocket, hoping to call Michael, but when she glanced at the top of the screen she saw she had no reception. She looked up to see that John had gone on without her; he had crept down the corridor and out of her sight. She cursed under her breath as she slipped the phone back into her pocket and then crept after him.

John had reached the desks and then continued towards a bend in the wall. The voices were coming from around the corner, and he stopped, pressing himself flat against the damp and rotting panelling. He took a couple of deep breaths as Amy sidled up alongside him.

'John,' she hissed. 'We should go. We should call Michael.'

'Just one moment,' he whispered. 'I need to see if it's her.' He bent his head slowly around the corner.

He could see what used to be a large open-plan office, although most of the furniture was gone, and what little remained was rotten and broken. Standing to the side he could see Sarah and another man; someone he didn't recognize. Her hair was shorter and darker than before, as they had suspected it might be; she was ready to leave the country under her Marie Mathews alias.

The man was wearing black boots, jeans and a leather jacket, dark glasses covering his eyes despite the fact that they were indoors at night. As he watched, he saw Sarah open her handbag, pulling out both the card reader and the small black card.

'It's them!' he whispered back to Amy without taking his eyes off the exchange. Then, the back of the man's head exploded as a deafening blast echoed throughout the structure. He slumped backwards to the floor, the card and reader falling from his hands.

Sarah span around, instinctively reaching into her handbag, but stopping as she looked up. Slowly, she raised her hands. There was obviously someone else there, someone John couldn't see.

Then he saw the man emerge from behind a wall. There was something familiar about him. It only took a second before he placed him. He was one of the Russians, one of The Devil's men, the one that Sarah had pistol-whipped. John knew he should run. He knew he should turn and run and get the hell out of there with his wife. But instead, curiosity got the better of him and he edged closer to get a better look.

The man had advanced until he was right in front of Sarah, his gun trained carefully on her. He was barking commands to her, something in Russian that John couldn't understand but Sarah could.

Slowly and carefully, Sarah lowered her handbag to the floor and then the man reached forwards, pulling open Sarah's jacket with his left hand while his right kept the gun trained on her. He was checking her, looking for other weapons.

Sarah's arms suddenly struck out, her hands moving in a frantic blur of speed. They knocked the gun to one side, although her assailant managed to keep hold of it. She kicked forwards, a powerful roundhouse kick that caught him in the stomach. It knocked him backwards and to the floor, but still he kept hold of the gun. There was another almighty bang as he fired again, Sarah diving to the side and out of the way. Then she was up and running, zigzagging between pillars and walls as the man fired repeatedly at her.

John could hear other gunshots now, some from up above, some from the far end of the building. It sounded like gunfights were breaking out all around them. The Russian was chasing after Sarah, exchanging gunshots as they went. The area in front of John was now deserted apart from the dead body lying on the floor. He turned. Amy was still there, standing a few paces behind him. She looked scared to death.

'Go!' he hissed at her. 'Get out of here. Call for help.'

'I'm not leaving without you.'

'Thirty seconds,' he said. 'I'll be right behind you. Just *go!*'

She turned, heading cautiously back towards the stairs and the way they had come in. John took a brief look left and right before he scampered towards the dead man lying on the floor. Even before he arrived, he could see what he was after. He crouched down, snatching the black smart-card from the floor. He was about to follow Amy when he saw a man emerge from a stairwell to his right. He had been spotted, and the man was raising a gun towards him.

John threw himself behind a cluster of old desks and chairs, even as a wooden chair next to him exploded from gunfire. He cowered on the floor behind the flimsy cover, desperately searching for something to help him.

'Come out,' came a voice, closer than he expected. It had a heavy Russian accent. 'Come out and maybe we'll let you live.'

Frantically, John searched around for something that could help him. But there was nothing of use here, nothing of value – just broken old chairs and desks resting on a mouldy rotten carpet. There were a few moments of silence while he searched and then he spoke up. 'I'm coming out,' he said. 'Don't shoot.'

His arms raised, he slowly stood up. The Russian was twenty feet away, his gun trained firmly on him. 'Come here,' he ordered.

John obliged, taking a few steps closer until the distance was halved.

'On your knees. Place your hands behind your head and put your fingers together.'

John did so, and the man came around behind him, the muzzle of his gun never losing track of him. He head the sounds of jangling metal, then the familiar snap of handcuffs being locked around his wrists. When he was happy that John was secured, he started to frisk him, searching all his pockets, taking out his wallet and checking its contents. When he was happy that there were no surprises, he reached into his own pockets, pulling out a thin black cloth bag. He pulled it down over John's head, and everything went dark.

The Russian marched him across the room and up a set of stairs to the floor above. With the sack over his head, John could see almost nothing, and the Russian had to keep helping him, annoyed at his inability to take directions when blind.

He was guided across the room and then shoved violently into a chair. Someone grabbed hold of his arms and he felt the handcuffs being removed, before they were replaced again moments later. He had been secured to the back of the chair.

'Don't go anywhere,' chuckled a Russian voice. He obviously found the comment funnier than John did.

From not very far away, John could hear shouting in Russian – loud, angry voices. Intermittently, he heard a female voice, sometimes swearing, sometimes shouting… and sometimes screaming in pain. He hoped it was

Sarah and not Amy, and hated himself for it. He prayed like hell that Amy had managed to get out of here and that help was on its way.

The screams and shouts continued for almost fifteen minutes, his hope of rescue gradually decreasing as the time drew on. Fifteen minutes of hell, sat in the darkness with the bag over his head, left to imagine what was being done in the other room to someone he cared for. And then… it all fell silent. He wasn't sure which was worse; he no longer knew if they were alive or dead.

He squinted as the bag was ripped from his head. After the darkness of the sack, even the torchlight being shone in his face was too bright. He was finding it hard to focus.

In front of him stood a thin man with a cruel twisted smile. There was blood on his hands and flecks of blood all over his face and shirt although he had no visible signs of injury. This was surely Victorovich, The Devil.

'We want the card,' he stated in a thick Russian accent. 'You know where it is, and you will give it to us.' In one hand he held a surgical knife. John could see blood on the blade.

This was it. This was how he was going to die.

'Tell me where it is,' the man snarled in his face.

'I don't know… honestly,' sobbed John as he looked down at the floor, unable to look the man in the face.

'Your lover… she kept her silence even as I tortured and killed her.' John's head snapped upwards as his brain processed the words. 'Yes,' the man hissed. 'I took great pleasure in taking her life myself. So really, there's no reason not to tell us. When it comes down to it, I don't believe you will have quite the same strength that she had.'

'Please,' begged John. 'I don't know where it is.'

'Bring her in,' barked the man, and an accomplice stepped out through the open door. He returned a moment later dragging a chair back with him, two legs scraping along the floor. There was someone sat in the chair, hand-cuffed to it, but even though there was a cloth bag over her head, John could still tell who it was; the shape of her body, her clothes… the wedding ring on her finger.

The man who had dragged her in pulled a pistol from his belt and read-ied it. Then he slowly raised the gun, holding it to the side of her head.

'How many people that you love have to die before you tell me what I need to know?' the man in front of John whispered into his ear.

'No, not my wife, *please*,' he whimpered. 'She doesn't know anything. She's got no part in this.'

The man just shook his head slowly.

John looked across the room at his wife. He remembered what Sarah had told him about these people. They had tortured her, and when she had been unable to tell them what they wanted, they had killed her. Now it was the turn of him and his wife, and he knew that they were never getting out of here alive. He knew with an absolute certainty that the man in front of him would never let either him or his wife go, even if he did give them the card.

It was time for a last stand. He had screwed up too much and this was his last chance to do the right thing. He just deeply, deeply wished that his wife could have been left out of this – he had never wanted to hurt her. At least it would be quick and painless, unlike it had been for Sarah. Their deaths would haunt him for the rest of his life… but that now seemed like it would be measured only in minutes.

'I don't know where it is,' John repeated, slowly and clearly.

'Three,' said the man as John squeezed his eyes shut, unwilling and unable to witness what was about to happen. 'Two... one...'

John heard a deafening gunshot ring out in the small room, and then the sound of his own screams.

Chapter 27

John's eyes jerked open. The man next to Amy had dropped to his knees, a gaping bloody hole in his back. Then, another gunshot echoed out and Victorovich flew backwards, staggering back across the room and falling to the floor.

'Fucking Russians...' spat a female voice. John looked across and saw that it was Sarah. She was standing in the doorway, cuts all over her face and torso and her top soaked red with blood.

'Sarah!' cried John. She was alive. He couldn't believe she was still alive.

She stepped over to Amy, pulling the bag from her head.

Amy blinked in the light and looked up at her, squinting. 'Fuck,' she muttered under her breath. 'I never thought I'd be glad to see *you*. I really thought I was going to die.'

'The day ain't over yet,' growled Sarah.

'Just let her go, and you can have it,' pleaded John. 'You can have the card.'

'Where is it?'

'Hidden. You'll never find it without me. But let her go and you can have it. I'll take you to it. I promise you. If I've ever meant something to you, please believe me.'

Sarah stepped forwards, kneeling down and frisking the dead Russian. She rummaged in his pockets where she found some keys and used them to unlock Amy's handcuffs. 'Go,' she said without looking her in the eye. 'Run as fast as you can and don't look back.'

'But, John,' she whimpered, looking back at her husband who was still handcuffed to the chair.

'He'll be fine,' Sarah smiled sweetly. 'But if I were you, I'd get going.'

Amy hesitated, still looking at John. 'I'll be fine,' he reassured her. 'But you need to go. Go call for help.'

'I don't have my phone. They took it.'

'Then find one. There'll be someone out there with one you can borrow. Just *go*, Amy, please.'

She looked at him with sadness and fear in her eyes. 'I love you, John. Come back to me.'

'I will. Now go.'

Reluctantly, she turned and left, running across the room and down the stairs. She didn't look back.

Sarah came over to John, looking down at him as he sat handcuffed to the chair.

'They told me you were dead,' he said stiffly.

'I think they still had further plans for me. They were trying to break you – I'm impressed you didn't crack.' She gave him a little smile, and despite everything it still lifted John's heart to see it. Then she crouched down next to him, looking at him on an even level. 'If I unlock your handcuffs, can I trust you not to do anything stupid?'

John looked broken and defeated. 'I promised you I'd let you have it if you let her go. You upheld your end of the bargain, now I'll do mine.'

'Where is it?'

'Downstairs. I'll show you.'

Sarah stepped behind him and unlocked the handcuffs, releasing him from the chair. 'Come on,' she said.

John stood up, stretching his arms and rubbing his wrists where the handcuffs had been digging into his skin. He looked across at Sarah. She was still holding the pistol in her hand. She wasn't aiming it at him, but he was acutely aware of its presence. She was keeping her distance too, not letting him come to close.

'Follow me,' he muttered. He led her down the stairs, over towards the area where he had seen them make the exchange.

He stopped as he came across another dead body on the floor. He looked like he might be another of the Russians, and was missing half of his face. Another victim of another bloody gun fight.

He nodded over towards the other body lying dead on the floor – the man she had given the card and reader to.

'Who was he?' he asked.

'Does it matter anymore?'

'I guess not,' he shrugged.

'Where is it, John?' She sounded impatient.

He pointed towards the cluster of desks where he had hidden from the Russian. 'Over there. Under the desk you'll find a panel in the floor – a patch panel for wiring up network and power sockets. It's in there.'

Sarah stepped cautiously over to the desk. Underneath, she could indeed see a floor panel; it contained four electric sockets and four computer network ports. She glanced back at John.

'It lifts up,' he explained. 'It's underneath.'

She knelt down, placing the gun on the floor next to her as she used both hands to lever the panel from its place in the floor. As she lifted it up, she could see the black smart-card resting on a pile of dusty cables.

She gave a sigh of relief, picking it up and holding it tight in her hand. Then she stood up, retrieving the gun and turning back to face John.

To her surprise, John was holding a pistol; he had taken it from the dead Russian on the floor. He was aiming it towards her.

'Put the gun down, Sarah,' he asked firmly. 'I don't want to shoot you, but I will.'

'What are you doing, John?' she asked gently, a look of confusion spread across her face.

'You've been lying to me the whole time,' he stated simply. 'All of this. This has all been one big lie.'

'What do you mean, John?' she replied, shaking her head in disbelief. 'I don't understand.'

'I know about you, Sarah. I know you're not working for MI6. You're not one of the good guys.'

Sarah took a step towards him, but he raised the gun higher, using both hands to steady his aim, and she stopped. 'That's not true, John.'

'Put the gun down, Sarah,' he said again, more forcefully this time.

She looked at him with an odd look on her face, as if trying to recall something. 'Upstairs,' she said slowly. 'When I rescued you and Amy… when

I saved your lives. Did you think I was going to *kill* her? That I was planning to kill *you*?'

John swallowed. 'Just put the gun down, Sarah. Please.'

'How could you think that, John? After everything we've been through, how can you think I would do that to you?'

'*Please*, Sarah.' He was pleading now. He didn't want to shoot her, but he thought he could if he had to.

She nodded, and then slowly placed the gun on the desk next to her. 'Just don't do anything stupid. This isn't what you think. You need to let me explain.'

'Someone who's *actually* from MI6 came to see me, Sarah. *He* explained the truth to me. He told me who you really are.'

Sarah shook her head again, but this time she had a smile on it. '*Really*, John? And you believed them? I wouldn't have thought you'd fall for that a *second* time.'

This time it was John's turn to shake his head. 'He had ID. He had a uniformed police chief with him.'

'And suddenly you're an expert on official government identification? You think you can tell a real police uniform from a well-tailored replica? From a distance?'

'Sarah…' started John.

'Did they take you in, John?' she continued. 'Did they take you into the MI6 offices? Did they even take you to a police station?'

He had to admit, they hadn't.

Sarah took a single step towards him. 'After everything we've been through, I can't believe you'd take their word over mine. You *know* me, John.'

'Don't come any closer…'

She took another step. 'I gave myself completely to you, John. There's nothing I wouldn't do for you.'

'I mean it,' said John as she took another step forwards, his voice start-ing to crack. He held the pistol firmly, still pointing it directly at her.

Looking him directly in the eyes, Sarah took another step, so that the muzzle of the gun was pressing into her stomach. 'If you don't believe me, John, then you might as well pull that trigger.' She wrapped her hands around John's as he held the gun tight. 'I love you, John. I want you, and after everything we've shared, if you don't want me… then you might as well pull that trigger, as I don't want to go on without you.'

Sarah felt the pressure against her stomach lessen.

'I'm… I'm sorry,' whispered John. The muzzle of the gun dropped, slowly lowering until it was pointing down towards the floor.

Suddenly John's arm was twisted backwards, pain shooting up his arm. His hand opened and the gun was snatched from it, whipped around so it was now pointing at him.

'Do you not remember what I told you?' she yelled at him. 'You should never aim a gun at someone unless you're willing to kill them. Were you really going to *shoot* me, John?'

'Sarah,' whispered John.

'*You* were going to shoot *me*?' she roared with added venom. 'You stupid fucker.' She raised the gun to point directly to his head. 'On your knees.'

'Sarah, don't do this,' pleaded John.

'*On your fucking knees!*' she screamed at him.

John nodded and slowly dropped to his knees.

Sarah moved around behind him and John felt the cold steel of a gun muzzle pressed against the back of his neck. It felt oddly familiar.

'Was any of it true, Sarah? All those little things you whispered in my ear. All the stories you told me. Was *any* of it true?'

'More than you might think. I really was a military contractor with Tom, but when I left I wasn't recruited by MI6. I was persuaded to go into a more lucrative line of work.'

'And did I mean anything to you?'

'Men…' she sighed with a shake of her head. 'You're all so easy to manipulate.' She gave a little laugh. 'The strange thing is, I did actually feel something for you, John, not just all those years ago, but the last few days too. I wasn't lying when I said there was a special place in my heart for you. It's just that… well, my heart isn't quite what it used to be. I was telling the truth when I said that I'm getting out, too. This card and reader will make me a very rich woman, but I'm afraid there's no place in my new life for a *Mr Hutchinson*.' She let out a tired and weary sigh. 'I've got to say, it's been good being with you one last time. I had fun revisiting the old days – you always knew how to make me happy, but all good things must come to an end. Say goodbye, John.'

'You fucking coward,' muttered John.

'*What?*' spat Sarah.

'After all we've been through,' said John. 'You could at least look me in the eyes if you're going to kill me.'

Sarah gave a little chuckle. 'I was trying to spare you. But if it's what you want…'

John felt the pressure of the gun disappear and Sarah moved around in front of him.

She lifted the gun, pressing the muzzle up against John's temple. 'Any last requests?'

'I suppose a last fuck's out of the question?'

Sarah tipped her head back and let out a laugh, a loud raucous belly laugh. 'Oh, John. Poor, sweet, horny John.'

'I did love you,' he said. 'Back then. If that means anything to you now?'

Sarah slowly shook her head. 'I'm afraid not. That was a long time ago. Several lifetimes ago.'

'Then Brand was right after all. You *were* just using me… and now you're ready to cast me aside.'

'Sorry,' she grinned. 'Time to say goodbye.' Then she pulled the trigger.

Chapter 28

There was a dull click.

'What the fuck?' she muttered. She pulled the trigger again; another click. The fucking gun was empty, all the bullets already fired. She swung her arm in rage, hitting John on the side of the head with the full weight of the gun and he toppled to the side with a cry of pain.

There was the slam of a door behind her, and she span around.

'Get away from him, you bitch,' hissed Amy from the doorway. 'I'm not going to let you hurt him again.' In her hands she held a gun, held out in front of her and pointed directly towards Sarah.

Amy squeezed the trigger, but the shot went wide, the kick from the pistol unexpected. Sarah moved quickly, trying to step behind John. He was on his hands and knees, and she grabbed him by the shoulder, trying to pull him upwards in order to use him as a human shield.

Amy's second shot was better. The bullet struck Sarah in the shoulder, spinning her around and sending her flying to the ground.

John pulled himself to his feet as Amy ran over to him. They stood side by side, looking down at Sarah as she lay on the floor before them, a pool of blood forming underneath her.

She looked directly up at John. 'It's not too late,' she croaked. 'I know you want me, John,' she appealed to him. 'Choose me, John. Stop her.'

He just shook his head. 'It's over between us.'

'You'll never hurt anyone again,' spat Amy. She pulled the trigger again.

Sarah's body spasmed once from the impact and then stopped. She lay on the floor, not moving. She was dead.

'Let's get out of here,' sighed Amy.

Epilogue

Twelve Months Later

John stood looking out the window of the Prague hotel, casting his eyes over the empty streets outside. There was the sound of gentle snoring from his bed and he turned to look at the naked woman sleeping there. They had checked in last night as Bill and Kate Thatcher: fake names with matching fake papers. Just an innocent couple on a weekend away in the Czech Republic.

He sat down at the small table by the window, the early-morning light seeping in through a gap between the curtains. A small black leather briefcase sat in the middle of the table and he opened it. Inside was a hidden catch and he released it to open up the bottom of the case and reveal a secret compartment within. It contained a small automatic pistol and a USB thumb drive, something he would guard with his life. He picked up the gun, double-checking it was loaded and ready to use, even though he already knew it was.

His attention was caught by something flashing out of the corner of his eye. It was his phone, a small LED on the corner flashing to indicating a new message. He put the gun back in the case, and then stepped across to pick up the phone and unlock it. It was updated orders. He checked his watch; the rendezvous had been pulled forwards.

He gazed again at the woman lying asleep on the bed, lying above the sheets in the warmth of the hotel room. He knelt down next to the bed, slowly running his fingers over her naked body, from the base of her neck, down her back and across her buttocks, until they reached her thighs where they lingered.

The woman rolled over, looking up at him with love in her eyes.

'I've had an update from Michael,' he said. 'The exchange has been brought forwards.'

'When?'

'Noon. It's taking place in Jankov, an hour from here.'

She sat up in the bed and glanced across at the clock on the wall. 'That still gives us plenty of time,' she purred seductively. She reached forwards, taking hold of him, pulling him down on top of her.

'I love you, Amy,' he whispered.

'Call me Kate,' sighed his wife with a wide devilish grin.

'Kiss me, Kate,' he said in a low hushed tone.

She did, and he was hers completely.

The End.